# MAROONED
## IN A STRANGE LAND

Book 1 of the Mind-Speaker Series

*To Mattie, Sol & Theo*

*Jim*

A Novel
by
James Dickinson

James Dickinson of Salt Spring Island
British Columbia, Canada
Illustrations & Cover Design by
James Dickinson

Canadian Copyright © May 15, 2017
Registration No. 1140489

ISBN: 978-1-77084-954-9

Printed and bound in Victoria, BC, Canada by First Choice Books and Victoria Bindery

To Ken

## Dedication

My story would never be published without the dedicated support of some very skilled people.

Judy, my wife, listened as I read and then revised each chapter.

Ken Fearnley, Jaqui Russin and Dennis Hayden took the time to review the book, offering valuable advice on possible revisions.

Helen Hinchliff and Marie-France Berube painstakingly went through the text as my copy editors.

Dr. Sue M. Scott, PhD gave her input as the final editor of my story.

My most sincere thanks to all the people who helped make this book possible.

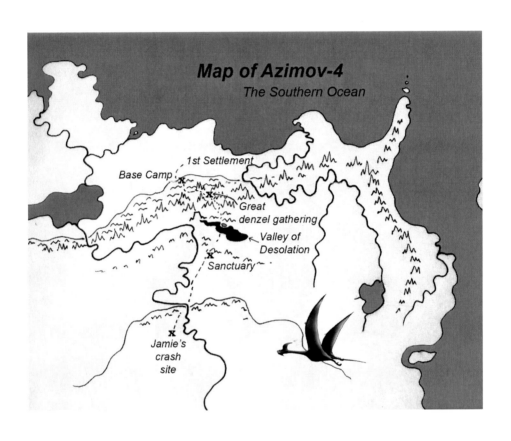

Map of Azimov-4

The Southern Ocean

Base Camp

1st Settlement

Great denzel gathering

Valley of Desolation

Sanctuary

Jamie's crash site

*The year 2126, Earth time*

# The Solar Storm

O n that fateful day everything appeared normal. They had the best of technology to explore this new land, what could go wrong?

Jamie was daydreaming as the mottled forest slipped by below them. His father banked their small craft into a tight turn and Jamie was pressed into his seat. Just as a clearing in the forest appeared ahead, the sun, low on the horizon, burst forth with blinding brilliance. It only lasted a few moments, but several things happened at once: the side of Jamie's face stung like a burn, he became weightless as the vessel abruptly lost altitude, his father struggling with the dead controls, and the nausea of seeing the ground coming up in a blur of green and purple.

*It was the searing heat and brilliant flash that woke Alheeza. As he blinked awake, the over bright sun was already fading back to its normal glow. Looking around the glade, nothing seemed out of the ordinary except for the spots in front of his eyes from the unexpected flare. What could have happened? The glade beyond seemed unharmed from the heat wave.*

*Feeling unsettled, he made a couple of turns about his sheltered spot. Out of the corner of his eye the shiny alien thing streaked past, hitting the ground and throwing up debris as it cascaded into the forest. Shredded foliage fluttered down through the cloud of dust that led to the shattered craft. Silence refilled the glade as he stared towards the mystery vessel, its once gleaming surface now scarred from the impact.*

*Time passed slowly as he sat waiting to see what the aliens might do. Perhaps they may have perished after the extremely hard impact with the ground. Alheeza had been observing these odd creatures for the past four sun cycles and nothing like this had happened. Just as he was about to give up and go to the stream for a much needed drink, he heard a slight thumping coming from the vessel. A narrow slit appeared along the clear portion, followed by a set of thin appendages. He heard more banging from within as the smallest of the pair clambered out, unsteady on its hind legs. As Alheeza watched from across the glade, the creature started uttering strange noises.*

Jamie swayed as he stepped away from the crumpled skimmer. The glade continued to spin, so he leaned back on the battered hover wing murmuring "Focus, Jamie, focus!"

Looking back at the skid marks left by the impact, Jamie muttered again, "What happened up there? One minute we were flying along and then that sudden flash! I thought we were going to die!"

Using one hand to steady himself, he reached up to probe his swollen cheek. "Oh shit that hurts!" he said to no one in particular. Looking down he saw that his jump suit was smeared with blood. When he rubbed his nose with the back of his hand he realized why.

Reaching up behind his left ear, Jamie touched the activation node of his embedded browser, asking, "Symone, what happened to us?" Not a sound came from the familiar synthesized voice, nor did his retinal imager appear. In disbelief he said again, "Symone, where are you?" In the silence Jamie felt the first stirring of real fear. Cut off from the full resources of their ship, how would they cope? He repeated the activation steps three more times but to his frustration all was silent. He staggered against the craft bewildered.

Suddenly, he remembered his father. "Dad, can you hear me?" he shouted as he staggered back to the cockpit. Grasping the damaged canopy, he heaved with all his might to open it wider. Metal scraped on metal, and suddenly the canopy slid open.

"Dad, are you all right?"

From within, Fingland answered weakly, "Jamie, take it easy, I'll be fine."

A few minutes later, a shaken, bruised and singed Fingland J. Chambers, crawled from the wreck and slumped to the ground gasping. Looking up at his his son, he asked, "Jamie, how are you?"

"I've just got a nose bleed and my face feels burned."

"Yes, my face is burned on one side too! But are you hurt in any other way?"

Jamie took a moment as he looked down on the blood streaked jump-suit before answering, "I feel like I've been beaten up by Robert's gang, but aside from that, no."

Fingland nodded his head, as he leaned back against their craft.

Spent, Jamie stared into the deepening shadows that stretched across the glade. In the silence that followed, he reminisced about the life they had lived. The trip to Azimov-4 had taken 19 years of earth time. Traveling at nearly light speed, their interstellar space ship had crossed the galaxy carrying almost 500 colonists with it. This small planet had held all the hopes of the political refugees escaping the horrors of the "Believers on Earth." Born on route, Jamie had never set foot on Earth, and his four weeks on Azimov-4 was his only terrestrial experience. From Base Camp he and his father, Fingland Chambers, had been sent on a survey mission hundreds of kilometers away. They were to collect information that would aid in the setting up of a self-sustaining colony. His parents had been among the scientists and other skilled professionals who'd hoped to escape to this new distant world. They'd kept him spellbound with stories about how they had managed to travel so far across the galaxy.

Touching the tender side of his face, Jamie looked out at the trench gouged by their survey skimmer, and wondered again what went wrong?

Fingland broke the silence. "What are you thinking about Jamie?"

Jamie shook his head as if that would clear his thoughts, "I was thinking about our situation. What caused the crash, and where did our burns come from?"

Looking toward the cockpit of their craft, his father took a moment to reply. "We seem to have had some sort of system failure. Let me check in with base camp to see what they know." He reached behind his right ear to activate his embedded browser. As he pressed the raised area under his hair line, he said, "Base camp, this is

Fingland, do you copy?" His retinal imager failed to come on. Feeling bewildered, he repeated his call, "Base Camp, this is Fingland, do you copy?" In frustration he tried again, "Margery, this is Fin, please answer me!"

More silence!

"Symone isn't working either Dad. What's going on?"

Fingland sat there with a far off look before saying in a low voice, "I can't reach anyone, not even your mother!"

Jamie's head spun, his stomach twisted, and his knees buckled. As the ground came up to meet him, he was vaguely aware that his father was also sick.

---

*The strange beings had survived the crash, but they seemed injured, perhaps dying. They had crawled out of their unworldly craft, uttered more of their strange sounds, vomited and then collapsed. Night was approaching and it was growing cold, but the young denzel pushed away his fears and crept closer.*

---

The first thing Jamie remembered was the sound of his own pulse throbbing in his ear, followed by a stinging on the burned side of his face. Somehow his senses told him that he was face down on the coarse ground cover. Lifting a heavy eyelid, bewilderment was replaced with shock as he met a pair of emerald cat-like eyes staring over a beaked snout. Fine scales glistened as they spread back over his delicate body.

The strange creature jumped back, spinning on its heel, and sprinted away from him with surprising speed. Forgetting his discomfort, Jamie levered himself up blinking in disbelief.

Later he would remember his first encounter with this creature in surprising detail. It was about the size of a large dog, but its front legs were longer than the back ones, giving it an odd look. The skin was shiny with ridges and it had spines along its neck and rump. It looked like a cold-blooded mammal, if ever there was such a thing. From the air they had seen all manner of creatures, but never anything this close or so bizarre.

---

All Fingland wanted to do was roll up and die; the vomiting had sapped all of his strength and he hurt everywhere. Darkness engulfed the glade and when he could finally draw a breath, he spoke hoarsely, "Jamie, go to our tulip shelter and get my sleeping sleeve, I'm cold."

"I've already pulled it around you."

"But…..I'm still cold." Fingland said with a shiver.

"The auto-temp is not working Dad"

"I should have guessed!" said Fingland.

"I know, Dad, what else should I do?"

"Remember all those nights back on Mayflower, when I would come to your bed and we would read through the old book together?"

"We talked about making a new life here, and you would show passages about wilderness survival. I always thought it was kind of a game we played."

Fingland looked around the darkened glade before answering, "Back then it may have been a learning game, but here it is very serious indeed."

Suddenly he was struck with another bout of retching.

Jamie crouched to hold his father's shoulders, unsure of what to do next. When the heaving stopped his father still shivered. Jamie slid him to a clean piece of ground cover, pulling the sleeping sleeve over his shoulders again.

Sitting back he wished more than ever that Symone worked. Going with his Dad on a survey mission had seemed not only a great adventure, but also a chance to get away from his tormentors back at Base Camp. Then things had gone so terribly wrong. Shivering, he looked around the darkened knoll ringed by giant flat-topped trees. The only light was the star field aided by the slim wedge of the small ringed moon about to set. He hoped the other moon would rise soon.

"Why has everything quit working?" he heard himself asking; otherwise, all was peace and quiet.

Then he heard what must have been some large creature crashing through the forest. The noise was coming closer and a chill of fear ran up his spine as he tried to imagine what was coming. From the air they'd already seen herds of large orange herbivores with great humped backs covered in rows of plate, their broad heads surrounded by a row of horns. Could it be them, or something worse?

As quickly as the disturbance started, it went quiet again. Jamie strained to hear, but all he could hear was a series of small clicks and tweets coming from around the glade.

He was just starting to relax when he heard a piercing yowl from the distant hills in the north. As the echoes died away, there was an answering cry, much louder. Jamie felt paralyzed as he waited for the next call, but it never came. As the small noises returned, Jamie huddled waiting for something terrible to jump from the shadows.

He shivered from the cold as it penetrated his thin layers of clothing. Before the crash they had retired to the comfortable safety of their well-lit tulip shelter. Inside they had enjoyed a savoury meal while talking about the new things they had seen from the skimmer. His stomach growled and he absentmindedly reached up to his Symone node, only to be reminded that it no longer worked.

The long minutes crawled by with the little forest noises gnawing at him and then the eastern horizon began to glow. Not long afterwards, a shaft of yellow moonlight spilled over the edge of the glade. At first, it give Jamie more courage but as he looked around the camp site, that too began to fade. He could clearly see the gouge in the soil from their crash, the useless shelter lolling open, and finally his unconscious father lying at his feet. Another wave of shivering shook his youthful frame. From his despair came a thought, perhaps a memory from readings with his father. His hand slipped into the utility belt that his mother had prepared for him, searching for the old jackknife.

---

*Alheeza crouched under a frond bush, its dense foliage quilted around him. After the terror of almost being touched by the strange one, he had raced back to safety. At first he wanted to return to his elders, but his curiosity still held him. Explanations could be made to them later.*

*The smaller one got up, and started to pick its way across the moonlit glade. It walked hunched over with its upper limbs wrapped around itself. It stopped at an outcrop of fluff brush. Alheeza was struggling to understand what he was seeing. In short jerking motions the being cut lengths of the brush not with its teeth, but with something held in its paw that flashed in the moonlight. It came to the denzel in an instant, these creatures modified their surroundings. It was amazing! His race could not pick up the shiny object to cut fluff brush even if they wanted to. What a revelation. But the question remained, where did they come from, how did they learn to use these things, and more importantly were there more of these creatures?*

*He carefully observed the young being as it made its way back to the other one still lying on the ground. Carefully it placed the bushy branches around and on top of the elder one. To his amazement it even stuffed the remaining ones under its wrinkled skin. He could never have imagined such a thing happening.*

---

Jamie felt a lot warmer now. Even his father seemed to sleep more contentedly since he had collected the fluff brush. Those that he had stuffed in his own suit were a bit itchy but that was far better than freezing in the open.

Meanwhile, he gazed about the moonlit glade, not sure what surprise might be waiting in the shadows. His parched mouth reminded him of how thirsty he was. How long had it been since they last had a drink, or food for that matter? He was imagining how good a fresh drink of nectar-aide would taste when he heard the far off crashing of a large beast again. Jumping, Jamie muttered to himself, "How could anyone get sleep in a place like this?" In that instant he wished he was back at Base Camp with both his parents and all the comforts he had taken for granted.

"What am I going to do?" he muttered.

Trying to push down his anxiety, Jamie refocused on memories of his wilderness studies. He could almost hear his father's words as he read from the old book, "It is truly said that the most important survival tool is the mind." Could the writings of Tom Brown over a hundred years before be applied here? The environmental studies so far indicated that the oxygen, carbon dioxide and water cycle applied to life here. It may look quite different from pictures of old

Earth, but with a clear head and a good deal of luck, maybe he could cope. It would have been nice for Symone to work, but his technology was no help now.

As Jamie sat there thinking, he stared up into the star field. Movement caught his eye; it was a good deal larger than a star and traveling at a steady speed. His father had pointed it out two nights earlier; the Mayflower, their interstellar spacecraft revolved around them every 68 minutes. As it caught the setting sun below the horizon, it looked like a beacon zooming overhead. The great ship had brought them here and it represented hope. And it made him feel a little better. As it passed into shadow on the eastern horizon, he came back to thinking about his father's condition. Absentmindedly, he reached up and rubbed the rash on his temple. It still stung but not as badly as it had. His father had a bigger patch on the whole side of his face. Was there any connection between it, the crash and the blinding flash just as the systems failed? The answer seemed just beyond his reach. If he could just focus he was sure that some insight might come out of it.

Then he remembered the damaged skimmer still in shadow under the overhanging flat topped conifer. Didn't it have emergency equipment? He picked his way towards the damaged vehicle.

It was dark in amongst the trees, his knee raked against an unforeseen protrusion. "Ouch, shit. That hurt!" he grumbled, as he picked his way more carefully along the side of the crippled craft, eventually finding the open canopy.

Behind the seats he found the thin outline of the emergency panel. It should have just popped open as his hand pressed the surface, but the systems were truly dead. Taking a couple of breaths he felt around more carefully. At the back edge, barely noticeable was a narrow protrusion. He tried pushing at it, nothing. Then Jamie pulled at the narrow ledge, nothing again. He took a couple of irritated breaths, and then on impulse he tried turning it counter clockwise. The young lad finally felt the lid pop up under his hand. Quickly, he pulled it away and reached inside. With a little more searching he grasped the handle, drawing the case out. It was heavy for its size. Being careful not to drop his treasure, Jamie clambered out of the skimmer making his way back into the moonlight.

The tangled plants seemed to grab at his tired legs as he trudged back towards his father. Fingland was sleeping fitfully when Jamie tumbled down beside him. The box was about 70 centimeters long and half that on each of the other sides. The interactive pad on the end was dark. "What a surprise!" he muttered to himself. Feeling carefully around the edge he found the small manual release, and was rewarded with a barely audible click as the end cap tipped open. The first thing that he pulled free was the medical intervention device. It too was inoperative. "What has happened to all of our equipment?" he moaned.

Inhaling with resolve, he reached into the pack again. This time he came out with a package. In the dim moonlight he could tell it was tightly sealed and he couldn't find the release. Then it came to him. Use the knife. As the contents started to spill out, he could just make out the shape of the energy wafers.

"Things are definitely looking up!" he said in a low voice.

After splitting the seal, he put a wafer to his lips. He had never tasted anything so good! Holding the rest of the morsel in the corner of his mouth; he dug deeper into the case. There were a few other objects that he could not identify but finally he came to the bottom and there were two rectangular containers. He carefully popped the seal and unscrewed the lid. They held some sort of liquid. Raising the rim to his dry lips, he took a sip. It was nutri-water and he gulped greedily until his thirst abated.

He placed the most precious of his treasures back in the emergency case and closed the lid. Next he knelt by his father noting his steady breathing. In the moonlight it was hard to tell what true colors were, but he thought his father looked very pale. Would he wake soon, would he feel better? Or if he was worse, what then?

# And Then They Were Gone

---

Jamie must have fallen asleep because he jerked awake to the sound of a distant yowl. He scanned the perimeter of the glade looking for any shadow that moved, but all stood still. The larger of the two moons had climbed well across the sky telling him that dawn would soon break. He reached again for Symone's node behind the left ear. "How long will it take for me to remember that doesn't work anymore?" he said out loud, shaking his head.

Jamie turned to look down at his father, who was now breathing comfortably. Should he disturb him? Jamie really needed to talk with him. Reaching down, he shook his father gently.

Fingland groaned.

"Dad, are you awake?"

"Mmmm……..m-maybe." he replied in a feeble voice.

Jamie dragged the emergency pack closer. Then he slid an arm under his father's neck lifting his head onto his knee.

"Dad, I'm going to give you a drink. Now be careful, we don't have much of this stuff."

He gave his father little sips, but Fingland coughed, spilling some of their precious nutri-water. Even so, his father looked somewhat better as he lay back down.

"What is all this stuff on me?" Fingland asked poking at the brush.

"You were getting really cold, so I used Captain Anderson's old Swiss Army knife to cut a bunch of this stuff to keep you warm," he said.

Patting his makeshift cocoon, Fingland winked: "Always thinking! Good going son, good going!" Plucking at a tuft sticking out of Jamie's sleeve, he continued, "And what is this?"

Jamie blushed with pride to hear his father's praise.

"Where did you get the nutri-water?" his father grunted.

"The nutri-water came from the skimmer's emergency pack. There is nothing working in the tulip shelter; in fact, none of the neuro-electronics are working!"

Fingland digested this last bit of news and finally said, "Can I have one of those wafers?"

As they sat in the moonlit nibbling on wafers, they gazed up into the star field. Over the western horizon a light appeared, moving quickly towards them. It steadily grew brighter as it came.

Fingland brightened, "Look, here comes the Mayflower again, right on time. She is our interstellar lifeboat, and a sturdier vessel there never was. I'm sure her crew are already putting our rescue on high priority. After all, it was Captain Anderson who got us all the way here from Earth. When it was my turn out of hibernation, I used to spend hours with him discussing our future here. For 19 years we traveled at near light speed. Now we are here and Earth has aged by centuries. You grew up onboard, while Margery and I took turns as parent. I can't imagine what it is like for you with all of the open country around us, especially after the confinement of Mayflower," said Fingland sounding a little stronger.

"I think I like it, except everything's gone quiet!"

Pride filled Jamie's breast as they continued to watch the starship speeding towards them.

Suddenly Jamie said, "Dad, we shouldn't be able to see Mayflower yet, it was too far from the eastern horizon to pick up the rising sun."

Fingland's jaw went slack at the implication. "Oh crap! You're right!" he said.

While they watched their ship streaking close, it suddenly burst aflame, leaving behind a luminescent trail. Time stood still as they watched the fire ball, and then it exploded. "Oh, shit! Oh, shit!" Jamie moaned.

Unseen by his son, Fingland's eyes rolled up into his head and he slumped sideways onto the ground. He did not hear the sonic boom that hammered across the hills minutes later.

*Not knowing what had awakened him, the young denzel looked up to see fire streaking across the sky. When it burst apart into many flames, he felt the screaming death of many! His eyes bulged from his quivering body as he stared into the now darkening heavens. What could have caused such a thing, and where did these feelings come from? Then deafening thunder crashed over him, making him shake with fear.*

# Marooned in a Strange Land

Jamie had not slept since the horror of seeing the Mayflower explode in the night sky. His gut twisted with the realization that the only home he had ever known had been ripped into incandescent particles. He wanted to believe it was just another asteroid that had happened by, but in his heart, he knew it was their starship. The place that he had grown up, all the lives that had touched him including Captain Anderson. Like  cold hands squeezing his neck, Jamie found it almost impossible to breathe.

*No it could not be happening! There must be some other answer,* a small voice inside seemed to say, but the Mayflower and all it held was gone forever.

Jamie screamed, "It's not fair! It's just not fair!"

Crouching beside his unconscious father, Jamie felt more alone than he'd ever felt before.

*After the star exploded, Alheeza couldn't sleep. The echo of many deaths still lingered in his body, but he was confused as to where the feelings were coming from?*

*His gaze was fixed upon the strange small alien that crouched beside its partner. Was it feeling hopeless? Surely it was his imagination. Communication of feelings was something only his race could experience.*

*Finally, thirst overcame his curiosity and he backed out of his hiding place to pick his way to the stream.*

Jamie's thirst had been gnawing at him off and on all night. Suddenly he pictured water, running water, a stream not far from here. Without questioning where the feelings had come from, he picked up the empty nutri-water container and headed for the edge of the glade.

Without hesitation he plunged into the darkened woods. For some unknown reason he seemed to sense the trail. It must have been at least a kilometer zigzagging through the tough undergrowth before Jamie found himself at the bottom of the hill. He could hear the running water before he could see it.

---

*Crouching beside the stream, Alheeza was deep in thought, when he suddenly felt as if he was being watched. He stiffened as he realized his folly. Being forever vigilant was their way of life. Slowly, he lifted his head to peer behind him.*

---

Jamie froze as he took in the same creature he had seen before. In the dappled moonlight, its shape was distinct. As if it sensed him, it slowly lifted its head, turning its pointed snout to look back at him. When their eyes met, it jumped into a defensive stance, mouth open, revealing evenly spaced small yellow teeth. A shiver ran down his spine as they gazed at each other. It stood about waist high at the shoulders. Its back slopped down to narrow hips, and a vestigial wing flap stretched from foreleg to shoulder.

Not looking away from those luminescent eyes, Jamie slowly stepped back up the trail, bringing his hands up, in a gesture of peace. Could this creature be dangerous? He hoped it was merely being cautious.

---

*Alheeza knew he should run, but his fascination with this alien held him in place. If it was dangerous, it should have attacked him while his back was turned. Now it held up its forelimbs and edged back up the trail. It stopped and started to make odd noises and gestures.*

---

"How can I communicate with you?" Jamie whispered.

He pointed to the creek, and then cupping his hand brought it to his mouth. Slowly, he repeated the gesture.

*What sort of behavior is this? Alheeza was making ready to bolt to his left, when an idea came to him. Could this strange creature be mimicking its way of drinking from the stream? He had to know, so he edged sideways ducking his head a couple of times in the hope this would be seen as some sort of understanding.*

Jamie was dumbfounded; the creature seemed to be acknowledging him as it stepped to the side of the stream. Jamie edged towards the stream, keeping as much distance as he could between them. He squatted by the stream, scooping a handful of water to his lips. He couldn't believe how good the water tasted. For a moment he forgot about the odd creature.

*Alheeza was fascinated by the way the creature used those little digits to manipulate his environment. What could his race do if they could pick things up like that?*

His thirst quenched at last, Jamie turned back, but the creature was gone. Was he imagining things? No, in the damp soil about him were clear tracks made by the three-toed being, which led back up the hill.

# Awake Again

The trail was easier to see as dawn pushed back the shadows. Jamie wrestled his way back through the brush, his head spinning from the night's revelations.

When he broke into the opening, he could see his father surrounded by loose fluff brush, sitting up clutching an open nutri-water container.

Running to join his father he panted, "Oh Dad you're awake again. I was so scared that you wouldn't wake up!" He knelt on the ground as the fresh tears formed.

"Jamie, you were gone when I awoke and I was so thirsty!"

Fingland looked off into the distance through bloodshot eyes. He reached a hand to his son's shoulder, "We should be going soon, don't you think."

Jamie stared at his father. Finally he said softly, "How, Dad? The skimmer is wrecked, none of our equipment works, and you've been so sick."

Fingland just looked out through the clearing towards the rolling hinterland to the north, its undulating forest catching the first shafts of morning light.

"They'll be expecting us back at Base Camp and we must get going."

"Dad, we can't even communicate with the colony. What are you talking about?"

Fingland made as if to stand. His legs quivering, he collapsed back to the ground. "I guess I need to rest a bit before we get started," he said as he reached behind his ear to activate his vis-com. Mumbling to himself he gazed at the horizon, allowing his hand to slide back to his lap.

Jamie tried again, "Dad, we need to talk about our situation."

His father said dreamily. "Base Camp will have everything we need. I'm sure they have sent out a rescue team already."

"That's what you think!"

"Yes."

"Dad, here's what I think: If our neuro-electronics have failed, couldn't Base Camp also be affected? I mean where is the rescue team, after all it only takes a couple of hours to fly here?"

"You sound so sure, but Base Camp has to be intact!"

"What do you mean, it has to be?" Jamie was talking louder than he intended.

"Surely, not everything could quit all at once. I mean, what would happen to us if that happened?"

A cold shiver ran up Jamie's spine as he looked at the man who had been his mentor. "Dad, are you feeling OK? You don't seem that good to me."

Fingland's head swiveled shakily towards his son. "Oh, I feel fine. I'm just a little tired."

This time Jamie did not answer his father, he just sat looking at him for the longest time. He noticed that the burn on the side of his father's face had changed color. It now was darker, like a maturing bruise, except that there was a set of blisters along his temple and down his cheek. It also ran down his neck and out of sight. "Dad, could you loosen your suit? I want to look at your shoulder."

Obediently, Fingland reached up to slide the suit seal open, exposing part of his shoulder. The disturbed skin ran just below his collar bone, and stopped. Jamie studied the pattern and then felt his own face. His burn seemed smaller than his father's. Could the side of the skimmer have protected them from the full blast? Whatever it was, it seemed to have cooked the neuro-electronics too.

Fingland muttered something about being tired. He lay back down, rolling over with his back to the warm morning sun. His breathing deepened almost at once.

While Jamie watched his sleeping father, despair swept over him. Fighting back his tears, he walked over to their useless tulip shelter. It had been their evening refuge after the long days of surveying the local area. Today the portable structure stood gaping open like some wilted flower. All of the self-sealing seams had released when the equipment quit and now it was useless.

Looking inside, his eyes came to rest on the M-G meal generator. Of all the things that had stopped working, it was this he missed the most. Once it was charged with its nutrient base, it worked for weeks. Now its dead interface was just another reminder that all their comforts were truly gone.

He cast his gaze around the sterile shell. The night before he had rummaged in their belongings to get their sleeping sleeves but now there seemed little he could find that would make any real difference. Then he spotted the corner of his great-grandfather's old fashioned book. Its faded cover and tattered edges beckoned to him from beneath his pile of clothing. Robert had tried once to take it away, and that had been the only time Jamie had struck back. His lucky punch gave Robert a bloody nose, but it cost him a black eye, cut lip and bruised ribs. In the scuffle, Robert forgot the book, so Jamie had won that battle.

Lifting it carefully, he cradled it lovingly to his chest. This was the book his father and he had shared so often, reading to each other as they practiced the ancient art of reading from a book. How he had loved those nights talking about making a new life on a distant land. They'd felt no need for a survival plan. They would solve every problem with technology. They always had before.

Part way across the glade Jamie perched on an exposed orange and grey rock, where he started to thumb through *Tom Brown's Field Guide to Wilderness Survival*. It had been a gift, handed down through the family. On his tenth birthday, his father had said, "This was your great-grandfather's book. Take care of it because there is no replacing it." He glanced at the publication date, 1983. "Jezz, this thing is old!" he said under his breath. He continued to thumb through the familiar text until he came to the chapter on fire. Of all the things in the book this had captivated him the most. On board Mayflower, he had never seen an exposed flame. Now with a second cold night coming, Jamie knew in his heart that their very survival might depend upon it.

The book described several ways to make fire, the first being the use of matches, whatever they were? It went on to outline friction as well as flint and steel. From his other studies, he knew about the use of a magnifying glass. Jamie squinted into the sun. "It might work," he said to himself. Rummaging in his waist belt, he felt around until his fingers found the glass disk. Like the book, it had been passed down through the family. He pulled it out, shifting it from hand to hand. As a child he had played with it, but none of the other kids thought it much of a marvel. Now, would it show its real value? Tom Brown had detailed all that was needed, but that was on Earth. Was it the same here?

Jamie had to find something light and dry to use as starter material. Tufts of fluff brush still protruded from the cuffs of his jump-suit. He plucked one from his left arm and placed it on the rock. The sun was now over the horizon and felt warm on his face. He experimented with the small glass focusing a spot of light on the edge of his tinder. It did not take long for a tiny spiral of smoke to rise from the fluff brush, stinging his nose and eyes. It burst into flame so quickly that Jamie jumped back from the rock in surprise. He could feel the sudden warmth from his tiny blaze, but almost as quickly as it started the little fireball dimmed and went out. A small clump of darkened ash was all that was left.

Jamie reached down to touch the still warm ash. Fire, he had made fire, but how to control it? A sudden thought raced through his mind, "I could have burned the whole glade!" he said out loud. This was going to take more care than he expected.

The itch had started just before dawn and he had ignored it since there were more pressing matters at hand. As he thumbed through the handbook the itch crept into his conscious mind. "Ouch!" he exclaimed as he bolted to his feet. The itch seemed to build and then it came again. "Ouch!" There was definitely something biting him.

---

*Alheeza shuddered in disbelief for the creature had magically created fire, right before his eyes. How could that be? His kind were deathly afraid of fire when it happened, as were all living things. He brought his attention back to the creature. As he was mulling over the implication of what he had seen, the creature started to slap at his body. The slapping became more animated, until it was literally dancing about. Then the most astonishing thing happened, it stepped out of its skin. The fluff brush fell away as the outer skin was discarded, exposing a pale white inner skin. Its body was surprisingly smooth, except for a tuft of fluffy stuff on top of its head.*

---

Jamie felt as if he was going insane as the itching and stinging intensified. His thin crumpled suit lay on the ground as he gyrated about trying to scratch and swat the irritated spots. He pulled off his under-trousers and as he did so a welt on his thigh caught his eye. Snatching up his magnifying glass, he peered more closely at the welt. There on the top of a red patch was a small writhing object. It was just a few millimeters long, magenta with yellow highlights. Jamie grasped it with his fingernails but he lost his grip. He tried repeatedly to pluck it off, but no matter how hard he tried to pull it off it seemed to embed itself further.

Jamie writhed from the escalating torment from these small invaders. He was going crazy.

---

*Suddenly, Alheeza sensed the anguish the creature was going through. Could it be the double-biters that lived in the fluff brush? If it was, then the only thing was for the creature to immerse itself in cold water to drive them out.*

---

For the second time in a day, Jamie felt as if he was struck by a thought that came from nowhere. He found himself running naked over the rough woolly surface growth and past the grasping brush until he flung himself into the icy stream. The cold took his breath away, but the torment seemed to ease at once. He let the frigid water wash over him as he lay face first in the stream. When he raised his head for a gulp of air, he noticed the strange creature watching him from along the bank. They held each other's gaze for a moment, then it turned and ambled into the underbrush.

As Jamie climbed onto the shore, the last of the frigid water dripped from his body. He shivered as his skin rose in waves of goose flesh, but the cold water had taken away the torment, leaving behind the fading welts. For the first time, he saw his multitude of fresh scratches from his dash through the woods. Some oozed a trickle of blood, but that was a small payment to be free of the parasites.

The way back up the trail seemed endless compared to his race to the stream. When he finally emerged into the clearing, the morning sun felt warm on his drying skin. "Best get a fresh suit," he said to himself.

---

*Alheeza was starting to wonder about his thoughts and the behaviour of the alien. Twice now he had been thinking about the needs of this creature only to have it act almost as if it had sensed his thoughts. That surely was impossible.*

---

When Jamie emerged from the defunct shelter, dressed in his last clean jump-suit, he found his father sitting up and looking around. An empty nutri-water container lay beside him.

"Dad, how are you feeling?"

"What has happened here? How did I get out into the glade and why do I hurt so much?"

"I helped you here after the crash…"

"What crash?" Fingland interrupted with a bewildered look.

Jamie was stunned and it took some time before he answered. "Dad, do you see that wrecked skimmer over there?" he asked. "We crashed into the ground as we were approaching camp last night. Don't you remember?"

Fingland Chambers swiveled his head taking in the ravaged ground leading to the crumpled craft and then back to their useless tulip shelter. Shaking his head, he said, "All I remember is flying back here and then I awoke stiff and sore in the middle of this clearing covered in this stuff. I don't remember anything else."

Jamie's mind raced trying to make sense of his father's memory lapse. Finally, he said, "Something happened when we were coming in for a landing: all of the systems failed, we crash landed cutting that deep groove in the ground, and finally stopped when it hit that flat-topped conifer. That's how you got hurt."

"We had better call this in," said Fingland as he reached behind his right ear to activate his embedded data base communicator. He pressed the raised area under his hair line saying, "Base camp, this is Fingland, do you copy?" He paused a moment, then repeated his call, "Base Camp, this is Fingland, do you copy?" He tried again, "Margery, this is Fin, please answer me!" More silence!

The cold hands of fear clasped Jamie, as he heard his father repeat the same message from the day before.

"That's funny, Jamie, the viss-comm implant isn't working. I can't seem to reach anybody, not even your mother!"

"Dad, you don't seem to remember, you went through all of this yesterday, word for word?

"No, I couldn't have. I'd remember that, I'm sure."

Jamie didn't answer his father right away as he continued to weigh his options. Then he went on, "We went through all of this yesterday after the crash. It looks like none of our support systems are working, not even Symone. They seem to have gone dead at the same time the skimmer crashed." He thought for a moment about what else to tell and decided to go on, "Last night when the Mayflower was orbiting over us, it entered the atmosphere and blew up. It probably killed all of those left on board. We are really in trouble here and I don't think there is anybody coming to help us."

Fingland's face turned pale and he fixed his bloodshot eyes on Jamie. "That can't be right! Surely there's another explanation."

Shocked at his father's denial, Jamie just stared at him. Suddenly, Fingland's body trembled again. Jamie was afraid his father would pass out once more.

Kneeling to put a hand on his father's shoulder, Jamie said, "I really need you to get it all together Dad, I can't do it all myself. We crashed, we got through the first night, and now we are alone. I need you to help me."

In a whisper, Fingland finally said, "I know you're a good boy

Jamie, and I can see the damaged skimmer over there, but I just draw a blank. He paused for a moment as tears welled up. "Why can't I remember things?" he asked. Then he dismissed the idea again. "This can't be happening; there must be another explanation."

Jamie's heart sank as he looked at his once vibrant father, the man who had taught him so much. "Maybe if I retell the story, step by step, providing more detail," he thought. His hands shook as he retold the part of how Mayflower exploded upon re-entry.

Jamie had hoped for a glimmer of memory, certainly some emotion, but his father sat unmoving for some time, staring off into space. Finally, he spoke again in a barely audible voice, "I don't remember any of that, but you were never a child that lied. Maybe it happened, but maybe your memory has been affected in some way."

Jamie was waiting for some conclusion from his father, but he just looked off into the distance. Finally, he said, "Help me up, I need to look around."

———————◯———————

*Hunger finally drove Alheeza to leave the glade. As he made his way to the Herman nut grove on the other side of the stream, he kept thinking about how the alien seemed to take action almost as if it sensed his thoughts. Putting that aside, he entered the tangle of interconnected branches that made up the extensive nut grove. Once inside he easily climbed the large descending branch, using his wide toes with their pointed nails to grip the soft skin of the tree. Stopping at the cluster of hard nuts, he lay down on the broad limb. Breaking open a node with his strong teeth, it exposed the rich meaty interior. This was one of his favourite foods.*

———————◯———————

Jamie led his father to the tulip shelter where Fingland seemed dismayed by its utter failure. The self-sealing seams lolled open to the sky, its internal systems lay dark and unresponsive. He hardly spoke as he went from component to component, poking at its dead interface. It was the same way at the crash site, only worse. Fingland picked his way around the edges of their slender craft ducking under the battered hover wing until he came to the cockpit.

He stared at the wreckage for some time before speaking, "How could I not remember this?"

Jamie felt sorry for his father as he watched him look over their once beautiful survey vessel. Finally Fingland crawled into the cockpit of the skimmer and started to examine it.

Jamie felt a wave of hunger and at the same time, it was as if he could taste some foreign food: firm, meaty, and tasty. An image popped into his head of a vast tree system that held within its tangled branches, clusters of the enticing food. Where had these images come from?

"What is it Jamie, you look confused?"

"Dad, I have to go check something out in the forest. You just stay here. OK?"

"I'm not so sure that is a good idea, maybe you should stay here, where I can see you."

"Look Dad, I'll be fine, just trust me." Jamie said over his shoulder as he made for the clearing.

Jamie followed the trail to the stream, where something ahead urged him on. After wading through the chilly water up to his knees, Jamie pushed his way past the tangled branches of an immense sweet smelling tree. It should not have been a surprise, but the strange little quadruped lay on a branch ahead. As the emerald eyes met his, the creature stiffened and grew larger somehow.

---

*Alheeza heard the alien approach the grove which made him freeze in position. The creature came through the tangled branches in exactly the same place he had come. The scales on his shoulder bristled as the creature approached.*

---

While they stared each other down, the raised protrusions along the creature's back seemed to relax. Jamie did not believe in coincidence, and this was the third time he followed a hunch, only to find this odd animal already there. Obviously, it had been eating from a nodule that had been broken open. Jamie's mouth watered at the thought of food, real food that could fill the stomach, not to mention abundantly available.

Moving very slowly, Jamie looked about the vast purple-green canopy of the tree. There were fruiting outcrops all around him. With great care, he stepped back reaching for a smooth branch overhead. With the ease of youth, he climbed the trunk and straddled a branch with a bulging node. He felt around the surface of it, noting how the lumps were so hard that he could not scratch them with his finger nail. "Time for the Swiss Army knife!" he said to himself as he drew it from his belt. After some experimenting with the longest sharp blade, he levered a node open. Sweetness filled his nostrils as he brought a chunk of the meaty center to his nose. He glanced over at the creature; it was still on its branch watching him. Slowly, he put the food to his lips and took a small bite. It was totally new in flavour, but he liked it. The nut, as he thought it should be called, was firm when bitten into but when chewed, it filled his mouth with a delightful flavour. All thought of the creature was lost as he took another bite and did not see it slip away.

By the time he left the grove, Jamie had eaten his fill and had his suit and waist belt bulging with more of the precious food.

Fingland worked his way around the craft, inside and out, trying to make sense of the damage. He was tugging on an inspection panel at the back of the cockpit, when Jamie returned. It was obvious from the young fellow's face that he was very pleased with something.

"Dad, you have to taste these nuts." said Jamie grinning.

Fingland climbed painfully from the cramped cockpit. He brushed his hands off and accepted the offered morsel. He chewed slowly and for the first time that day, Fingland smiled saying, "Where did you get this?"

"I've been exploring in the forest, and I saw a creature eating some of these. I thought, if it was good for him, then maybe we could eat it too. So far I feel fine and the hunger is gone."

Jamie did not try to explain the funny feelings of insight that led to the nuts. Was it coincidence that helped him find water and food at exactly the same time the creature was there, or was something else happening? His mother often had times when she seemed to be reading his mind. That was a family joke, but what was happening here?

He held out another portion of the meaty nut to his father. They stepped out into the sunlight and sat together on the rocky outcrop, where the morning sun felt warm on their faces. Fingland asked Jamie to tell him once again everything that happened since the crash, adding as much detail as he could, including his survival tactics. When Jamie had finished, they sat for a time looking out over the rolling hills.

"My memory is still a blank, from before the crash until I woke up here in the clearing. All that you told me must have happened as you describe it. I just can't understand how everything could have quit all at once." Fingland reached up probing his useless viss-comm, and then went on. "Last night must have been a terrible time for you. If it really was the Mayflower last night burning on re-entry, things could not be worse. Captain Anderson was like a brother to me, not to mention the rest of the crew. The whole thing seems so unreal. Not that I don't believe your story, it's just that I don't remember any of this myself."

"It is really hard for me Dad, you were awake and talking to me, but you can't remember anything. I don't know how to make you understand, but there is no other explanation for what I saw and felt last night. Look at us now, we are all alone here and nothing works. Doesn't it make sense that Mayflower suffered the same fate?" said Jamie as his throat tightened again.

Fingland looked at his son, who looked years older somehow. He went on, "You're right! I don't think I could have done nearly as well as you did last night. I really have no idea how you did it without help. That's really quite remarkable, and you say it was our old book that helped you get through it!" He looked at his son's face with its fresh scratches and fading burn. With pride he continued, "I know you are almost seventeen but I feel like I have missed you growing up."

Jamie blushed and after a moment he said, "You were so sick last night Dad. I thought you were going to die," His voice cracked as he looked down at his feet. "It was really scary."

"But look at what you did for both of us, I couldn't be more proud." said Fingland as he reached over hugging his son.

They clutched each other in a long embrace and finally Jamie said, "I have to show you one more thing."

Leaving his father he walked a few meters to the stand of fluff brush, and cut several pieces of the dry plant. Back at the edge of the rocky outcrop he stripped the tinder from its stems and placed it on a wide flat rock. With a flourish, he produced his lens, adding, "Now watch this!"

In the bright sunshine, it only took a few moments focusing the magnifying glass to create a small spiral of smoke. Poof, it burst into flame! Jamie glanced up at his father's astonished face.

"Now that is amazing!"

Jamie added the stems to the fire. "We have to be careful though, the fire must be made where it will not burn out of control."

"Wow!" was all Fingland could say.

"I think we'll be much warmer tonight, don't you think?"

They took turns adding small bits of dry foliage to their little fire. Jamie pulled out his old book, showing his father the chapter on fire.

"Remember this Dad; we used to wonder what it would be like to sit by a real fire. Now we know. Isn't this great?"

Fingland just smiled looking from his son to the fire before them.

"I am really tired, Dad, I have to lie down for a bit."

"OK, son, you just curl up here in the sun while I read parts of this book."

Jamie was asleep in moments.

---

*The young denzel was sound asleep too, hidden well under his favourite yellow fan bush. He twitched as a dream took hold of him. The alien stood before him, its unblinking pale blue eyes locked onto his. Within his head, it spoke to him. It seemed perfectly natural to hear its thoughts.*

# The Second Night

J amie awoke with a start, the dream still lingering. He looked about the glade expecting to see the strange quadruped standing nearby. The way it had been speaking to him telepathically had seemed so real, as if it had just happened, not a dream at all. He shook his head muttering, "This place is starting to drive me crazy. Not hard to understand why…."

The crackling sound behind him brought him fully alert.

There in a depression alongside the rocky outcrop, his father was kindling a small fire that snapped and popped as he fed it dried twigs and stems. When he heard Jamie move, Fingland looked over his shoulder as a broad smile spread across his blistered face. "Look what I did while you were sleeping. This *Field Guide to Wilderness Survival* is really amazing. What luck that you brought it with you on our expedition."

His father went on, "I saw clouds building up in the west and remembering what you told me about starting the fire, I thought I had better get a little one started before the sun lost its power."

Jamie nodded, "That's my Dad, thinking ahead." He felt a weight lifted off his shoulders as hope started to replace the despair of the previous day.

*Alheeza awoke, smelling the rain on the wind, time to take shelter.*

Jamie turned his attention to the sky. A blast of wind lifted his hair as he steadied himself in the gusts. The sky was quickly darkening with billowing clouds rolling towards them. He had the strangest sensation that he knew what was coming, even though his conscious brain knew this was impossible.

Fingland was watching his son's face, there was a troubled look about him and he said, "What is it Jamie, you look worried all of a sudden?"

"It's that funny feeling again, the same one I had with the water and the nuts. I just got this sudden urge that we'll need shelter tonight because...." he trailed off again looking up at the darkening horizon, "because it's going to rain!"

"Rain, how do you know that? We have never seen it rain here."

"I don't know; it's just a feeling and I'm starting to listen to these feelings. Look, Dad, I know this sounds really weird but I think we should do something to stay dry if it rains. The old book has some options but I don't know if we'll have much time before the storm."

"Why can't we just use the skimmer or the tulip shelter?" his father asked looking about.

"I was thinking about that last night. The canopy on the skimmer won't close anymore and...," he turned looking at the useless tulip shelter, "and the automated shelter has failed with no hope of reactivating it. We need to get our extra clothes into a dry place. Is there anywhere in the skimmer where they can be stuffed?"

Without seeming to be aware of how their relationship had changed, Fingland Chambers got to his feet and strode off to the shelter. Jamie sat there for a few minutes fingering his multi-purpose knife. He looked around them and then back to the shelter. It was made up of six identical broad sections that tapered to a point. Before the system failures, they had automatically sealed to each other, making the bulbous structure robust and weather tight. Now it lolled open uselessly, as if to catch as much rain as possible. He looked back down at his knife and made a decision.

---

*Alheeza hadn't slept much in the last five sun cycles and as he nestled into the soft dry fronds beneath a thick canopy of the ulland, he knew he was going to sleep long and deep. Not even the wilda-cats would be out in the downpour to come. His mind wandered back to the strange creature that walked on its hind legs.*

29

*His fascination with it was unmistakable, but he had to be cautious. After all, it was an alien and could be dangerous.*

———————————◁▷———————————

Jamie tested several of the blades from his Swiss Army knife on the tough dura-fiber of the shelter. The serrated blade sawed though the synthetic weave the best and before long a complete section lay on the ground.

Jamie was stripping a thin neuro-fiber from along the edge of the second shelter section when he heard his father approach. "What are you doing here Jamie? You are wrecking our shelter."

"Well, I decided that since all of the neuro-electronics are dead, this unit is expendable. I wanted to see if these sections could be used to make a quick shelter for tonight."

Fingland looked down at his son. "This is totally irregular. I am sure that Base Camp's tech help could have fixed it, but now it is useless."

Raising his voice in frustration Jamie said, "Tech help! Are you serious? Since none of our viss-comms work anymore, how exactly are we to get tech help?"

A puzzled look came over Fingland and he seemed to be searching for an answer.

"Dad, just help me drag these over to our fire pit, OK."

"All right, but...." He trailed off, before dutifully following Jamie back to their campfire.

"Oh, the fire is almost out!" exclaimed Jamie as he got down on his hands and knees to examine it.

"The book said to blow on it and add more of the small tinder," his father suggested.

Jamie blew on the coals, raising a cloud of ash and smoke. He coughed drawing back with his eyes stinging. As the smoke cleared he could see the coals were still smoldering. This time he blew a little less enthusiastically and was rewarded with a red glow with less smoke and ash. Carefully, he dropped a few branches onto the coals and blew again. They didn't catch, so he pulled the larger bits off the coals and added some fluff brush. This time when he blew gently on the dwindling fire, the flames caught and he was able to add a little fuel at a time until there was a generous fire.

When Jamie stood, he was shocked to see how fast the storm clouds were approaching. The sun was blotted out, sending a chill of apprehension up his spine. He staggered as the first gusts whipped his hair about his head. Time was running out, they needed to get shelter. Turning back to the two white sections of dura-fiber, Jamie struggled to see how he could set up the shelter so that it faced away from the wind thereby protecting them and the fire. Stepping forward he pulled one unit towards their fire pit. "Dad, take the other end and hold it for me."

Fingland took hold of the slim end. The wind was working against them. Fingland looked around and said, "We need some way to secure it, don't we?"

Jamie looked up, "Yeah, I know. We don't have any real tools and it's hard to attach this to anything." Suddenly, he wasn't feeling all that confident as he realized his seventeen years weren't giving him all answers.

He dropped his end and started to walk around the area, not really sure of what he was looking for. His mind whirled as he tried to think of what options were available to him. At the back of the rocky outcrop, there were a number of rock fragments strewn about in the woolly surface growth. Quickly, he tossed them towards the tulip sections and then stood for a moment considering his options. To the side, his father had piled a good deal of fire wood. Among the branches were several longer pieces. He tugged these free and studied them. "It might work!" he said to himself. Using his knife, he cut a branch to about shoulder height, leaving one end pointed. Drawing the two wide sections of the shelter together he punched a hole in the corner of each one. Using the neuro-fiber, he bound the corners together and poked the stick part way through.

"Dad, help me hold these in place." The wind tugged at the unit as Jamie struggled to tie a rock to the end of the cord. "Put a rock on that corner and then help hold down the other end."

Fingland stood frozen in place, staring at his son. Jamie looked up as he finished placing his tethered rock. "What is it Dad?"

"You do not say please anymore. Where are your manners?"

"Oh Dad, I am sorry! It's just that we really don't have any time, the storm is almost here! Please help me!" Jamie pleaded.

It was as if the storm had timed its entrance to Jamie's last statement, the wind gusted, bringing with it the first of the large rain drops. Jamie could feel the back of the shelter start to lift with the higher winds. "Dad, quickly put a couple of rocks along the back. And hurry please!"

Fingland bent to his task, while Jamie secured the last corner. Before ducking back in, he stopped to toss their fuel under the protective edge of the new shelter.

"Come on Dad, let's get into this before we get really wet."

Fingland stood for a moment more looking up at the storm. A wall of grey was closing on them. Within it, a bright flash struck a nearby hill, followed a few moments later by a resounding crash. "What the hell was that!" he said using an uncharacteristic euphemism as he swung under the shelter.

"Thunder and lightning!" Jamie replied. "I read about it."

Fingland looked wide-eyed as the deluge began, but for all his book-learning even Jamie was stunned by the driving rain and gusting winds. When there was a lull between the gusts, it felt as if a great tap had been turned on delivering a smashing wall of water down about them. Had the fire not been under the edge of the shelter, it would have been doused in moments. Lightning suddenly brightened the gloom again, allowing Jamie to observe water running everywhere while puddles were forming in the hollows. Small streams snaked along the edges of their lean-to, but he noticed most of it was draining away. In an instant, it was dark again and thunder crashed around them.

"How could this get worse?" his father hissed.

As if in answer to his question, white balls started thumping down around them. Jamie reached out to pick one up. "It's ice Dad, ice falling from the sky! Did you ever see anything like this back on Earth?"

"No, we lived inside the company facility. We never thought about what was going on outside."

"But you came here looking for a better life, a place where the Mayflower Colonists could start over again."

Fingland hunched closer to the fire, then stared out into the storm, "Back on Earth, the True Believers were taking over everywhere. Opposition leaders would vanish in the night, never to be seen again. It was a terrible time in our history and we didn't pay much attention to the weather outside the domed city. It seemed unimportant. What was important was planning our escape to here."

# Misty Morning

———————◇———————

Jamie awoke curled in front of the ashes of their long-dead fire. For a few moments, he took in his dim surroundings. Everything was shrouded in fog. Water droplets clung to the woolly ground cover that protruded from the numerous puddles.

Through his damp clothing, he felt a deep chill that seemed to stiffen his whole body. With a grimace, he opened and closed his stiff fingers. Carefully he stretched, only to find that he hurt everywhere.

Fingland stirred behind him groaning. With an effort, Jamie levered himself into a sitting position to better see his father. His face was contorted in pain or maybe it was just the burn stretching it into a permanent scowl. Despite his facial expression, he was sound asleep and Jamie didn't have the heart to wake him.

Some water had pooled within the shelter but it was amazing how well they had weathered last night's storm. He looked around, becoming aware of the silence. It was so quiet that all he could hear was his breath and the occasional drop of water falling from a leaf nearby. There was none of the clicking or squeaking that had made up the normal background symphony.

It was hard to tell what time of day it was. The sun was making the fog glow, but there was no warmth from it this morning. He took inventory of what was at hand. Thankfully, he had tossed the full water container and the collected nuts into the shelter when they started to build it the night before. It was not a hearty breakfast, but as he washed down the meaty nuts, it went a long way to reviving his spirit. His father stirred and opened his eyes.

"Oh, Oh!" was all he said as pain traced across his face again.

"Take it easy, Dad, I was stiff and sore when I tried to move too."

"I'll say!" groaned Fingland as he lifted himself on one elbow.

Jamie handed him the water and nuts. They sat quietly staring into the gloom. Finally, Jamie broke the silence, "Do you think Mom's all right?"

"I hope so. Your Mom is one of the smartest people I have ever known, and if anyone can cope with a crisis, it's Margery. I wish she was with us now!"

"Dad, do you remember how you used to tease her about her ESP? Somehow, she knew or guessed what I had done or sometimes what I was thinking."

Yes, it was our family joke. Why?"

"I was just thinking is all….." Jamie trailed off, but he was still thinking about the forest creature and the coincidence of their meeting just when Jamie's needs were at their greatest.

Jamie absentmindedly rubbed his inoperative viss-comm. Then he had a thought: "What if we were to walk back to Base Camp? I wonder how long that would take?"

"I don't know if that is such a good idea. In all the training, it said that we should stay with our downed vessel. It helps the rescuers to find us."

Jamie looked at his father in disbelief, "What are you talking about? If Base Camp was hit too, there will be no rescuers!"

Shaking his head, Fingland replied, "I don't know if we should risk it, after all, we still have all our equipment here and maybe they will restart."

"Restart? Are you serious?"

"Now don't get upset, we have to be careful about what we do next."

"Upset!" Jamie said louder than he intended. "Dad, we almost died in that crash. We have no idea why everything quit all at once! I saw the Mayflower explode overhead, and you want to wait to see if everything just starts on its own again?"

"All right, just calm down. Remember our technology has never failed before; historically, computers were fixed by shutting them down and restarting them. Maybe that is what is happening back at Base Camp. Anyway, the manual said to stay put," Fingland answered in a steady voice.

Jamie thought for moment and in a level voice answered, "Dad, that manual assumed that the crash was an accident. What we are talking about here is a total failure of all our thinking machines. Every neuro-electronic unit is dead. That goes way beyond what the manual tells us to do!"

Fingland just stared at his son, who had never spoken to him that way before. He stopped and looked around the sodden glade with their ruined equipment. With a quiver in his voice he went on, "I never thought something like this was even possible. I have no plan that will get us out of here. I am so sorry."

"I'm sorry too! I did not mean to get upset with you. I am really scared of what will happen to us!"

"I can understand that. To answer your first question, it took us two earth hours to get here from Base Camp. That is about 600 kilometers. How far do you think we can walk in a day through the wilderness? You watched as we crossed mountains, waste land, forest and rivers to get here?

Jamie screwed up his face and then went on, "I know that sounds impossible but we have to try. Trying is the only way we will know. After all, if they were going to rescue us they would have been here the first night when our signals failed."

"You have me there. OK, maybe it's not so crazy to walk out of here."

# Into the Unknown

A s the sun burned through the fog, tendrils of mist rose from the ground cover. Jamie tromped through the soggy glade checking to see if they had overlooked anything that might be useful on their trek.

By mid afternoon, they'd collected their meagre supplies, arranging them on the rock in front of their shelter. Jamie stood with one hand on his hip while browsing through his survival manual. Fingland looked over at him while absentmindedly scratching at his chin stubble, "Can you get more of those nuts before we leave?"

"I was planning on doing that next," said Jamie as he pulled out his jackknife. "I think this is the only sharp steel item we have. I'd better not lose it." With that he headed off into the brush.

Starting the fire was far more challenging with so much rain the night before, but by the time the sun sank in the west, they had turned a smoldering fire into a cheery little blaze. The sky was clear and after the first moon went down they stared up into the sky. At first, neither one mentioned the absence of the Mayflower passing overhead until Fingland spoke up, "I've been watching for the ship, hoping you were wrong but it isn't there anymore! About 225 were to be sent to each colony. Ours was the first to deploy. Depending on when the second colony was able to get settled on the other side of Azimov-4, there could be as few as 50 crew members still on board. Your mother came close to staying with the science team on Mayflower...." He trailed off and then added, "I hoped you were wrong, but I fear you are right and they are all lost..."

Jamie's throat was tight as he spoke, "I can't believe I'll never see Captain Anderson again. Like you, he encouraged me in my studies with old books and ancient technology."

They'd been sitting staring up at the star field when Jamie sensed movement in the eastern sky. There was a whistling sound as the shadow drew near. A huge dark winged object streaked overhead, vanishing beyond the palisade of flat-topped conifers. In just a few heart beats the silence was split with the most terrible scream, followed by thrashing and shrieking. As quickly as it started, the ruckus stopped. Only the rhythmic beat of huge wings could be heard departing into the west.

"Holy Shit, what was that?" Fingland swore, failing to notice the look of terror etched across Jamie's face.

---

*Moments before, Alheeza had been speaking to his genetic elders, summarizing in mind-speak fashion his observations of the ways in which the aliens differed from them. Most important, he thought, was the way they could pick objects up and manipulate them. But the attack came with extraordinary speed. One moment, he was detailing the idiosyncrasies of the strange beings and in the next the screaming winged creature had burst down upon them, its razor talons snatching each of the elders, hoisting their shrieking bodies into the sky. The air was filled with the stench of rot as the night terror's wings thundered, lifting its victims away.*

*A terror unlike anything Alheeza had ever felt ,sent him crashing through the underbrush, heedless of its obstacles. He had never seen a Great Raptor before, but he knew exactly what it was. Death from above had visited his family, and now he blindly plunged towards the glade.*

---

Jamie could hear his heart pounding in his ears, as fear welled up from his stomach. He knew in his heart that something or someone had just died. Could it have been his four-legged friend, he wondered?

Standing next to his father, he strained to hear the last beating of the giant wings as the winged creature flew eastward. Then nothing moved and the silence grew. Suddenly, something came crashing through the bush toward them. It wasn't big; nevertheless, as it emerged from the trees, it startled Jamie. Then it stopped nearby, its large eyes reflected the yellow light of their fire.

Jamie's panic started to drain as he recognized the intruder. "Dad, I think that's the strange animal I was telling you about!"

In a low voice Fingland asked, "How do you know, we can barely see it?"

"I'm sure that's him."

After a pause Fingland added "What do you think happened out there?"

"I don't really know, but I think something died a terrible death and I think this creature witnessed it!"

"Mm-hm." was all that Fingland could add.

After a short while the creature backed part way into the trees, but its yellow eyes could still be seen watching them.

———————————————

*Back in the shadows of the brush, Alheeza watched the aliens as they added branches to their fire, building up a sizable flame. He had this irrational feeling that somehow he was safer near these aliens, with their uncanny ability to make fire, than out in the woods where the smell of death still lingered.*

*He watched the star field, expecting to see another winged shadow coming for him. He had never felt the loneliness and isolation of being left without the mental link with his genetic elders. They had been preparing him for his adult life, but they still had so much to teach. The way they touched his mind with their gentle thoughts ,was always a comfort.*

*The aliens took turns building up their fire and dozing in shifts. Finally the glorious rays of the rising sun split the shadows of the glade. Alheeza rose and trotted to the stream.*

———————————————

"I still don't know if it is such a good idea to walk off into the wilderness without proper equipment." Fingland stated as he looked into the sleeping sleeve that held his few possessions.

"Look, Dad. We have a choice to make. Would you like to try to find out what happened to Mom, or do you prefer waiting here on this hill until that flying thing comes to kill us too?" Jamie asked. This time he did not feel badly about being so bold about their stark choice.

Fingland looked at his son, his eyes widened with disbelief, "I'm not sure I like your tone!"

"When are you going to see what's happening around us? We have not been rescued like the manual says! We have no idea what has happened to Mom at Base Camp, and I'll bet they've lost their systems too. They are probably deaf, dumb and blind without neuro-electronic technology. And yes, I am upset about the loss of it too; I miss Symone the most!" Jamie answered hotly.

"OK, OK, you've made your point. I'm scared to leave here, but you're right. It's just as dangerous to stay."

There was little said after that. Jamie looked into his own sleeping sleeve. It contained: his survival book, one drinking container, two pairs of jump-suits, several handfuls of nuts in clear sealer bags, four pairs of under trousers, four nutri-wafers, several bandages, a solar blanket, and disinfectant. Around his waist was the belt with its pouches carrying the most precious of his items: his Swiss Army knife, magnifying glass and an old spoon. It was not much to head into the wilderness with, but it was all they had. His father carried the same clothing, food and water.

Fingland looked around the glade that had been their camp for these past few days, and then he looked north. "How do we find our way in the forest, Jamie?"

"In my foraging, I found there are animal trails through the brush. When we reach hill tops or openings, we use the sun to keep our bearings." Jamie turned and trudged off toward the edge of the hill.

Fingland said, "What about a cloudy day?"

Jamie just kept walking towards the trees where a flock of large, yellow flying creatures lifted into the air, screeching as they flapped upward. Jamie looked up as they passed overhead, suddenly several soft turds landed at his feet. "I suppose you could call that an omen!" Jamie muttered.

The animal trail eventually led through clumps of three meter high brush with long, slim, silvery leaves. Jamie could hear his father crashing along behind him as he ducked and pushed branches aside.

"Are you sure this is a good idea picking your way through this growth?" he could hear his father call from behind him.

Jamie just kept walking. How could he know if it was a good idea? Nobody had ever tried this before.

---

*Alheeza decided that following the aliens was his only option. The emptiness he felt inside after the loss of his genetic elders gnawed away at his concentration. Until he found a secure shelter, he was still vulnerable from the Great Raptors at night. Despite the wisdom of his race, none knew why they came to kill every 15 season cycles, and it was growing worse each time.*

*The odd creatures seemed to be leaving this area, and since they were headed in the general direction of the great denzel gathering, he would follow for now.*

---

They walked for a couple of hours and when they emerged from a thicket, Jamie caught a glimpse of something that did not fit the terrain. A torn section of charred metal protruded from the surface growth.

Fingland dropped to his knees, stroking the fragment, calling Jamie to join him.

Jamie looked at the metallic chunk, with its melted edges and scorched surface. Its underlying construction could still be seen. It was a bulkhead section. There was only one place that could have come from—the Mayflower.

Fingland started to weep. "They're all gone," he moaned. "All of them." He paused, and then he whispered, "Now I know: we really are marooned."

# First Camp

———————◯———————

Scratched and foot sore, father and son stopped for the night in a clearing. They had passed two small streams, where they refilled their water containers. In the early afternoon they had come upon a large nut grove where they collected as much as they could carry. In honour of one of the scientists from the transport ship, they named the fruit Herman nuts. Even Fingland had seemed to come to life as they collected the readily available food.

As they made their way from thicket to nut grove, the forest was filled with more noise than Jamie remembered. Mostly, it was the many small creatures going about their lives, but every once in a while, they were startled by distant crashing and once they heard a far off bellowing. Jamie had been hoping that once they left the glade, the journey would lighten their spirits; instead, he was growing fearful.

Open spaces were far scarcer than he supposed, so that by the time they found a suitable camp site, it was late in the afternoon. The sky was clear, but the sun was too low on the horizon to use the glass to start their fire. Night was coming and they needed a fire. Jamie looked about the area as a sense of desperation started to build.

"What are you thinking?" asked his father.

"I can't get a fire started Dad. The sun is too low…" Jamie trailed off.

"What does the book suggest?"

Jamie sat cross-legged on the ground, pulling his survival book out. Tom Brown's passage on iron and flint had been a favorite and there was an illustration showing sparks showering off the back of a knife rapped on a rock called flint. He wondered if any rock would do.

"Dad, maybe you can look for some rocks while I gather some tinder and fuel. We'll have to hurry; it'll be dark soon."

Fingland returned with rocks of differing sizes and colours. As his father watched silently, Jamie knelt down near the fire he'd laid and tried rapping his knife blade across each stone. But he failed to get a spark. Exasperated, he stood up exclaiming, "Damn it all anyway, I wish it was easier than this!" Unable to control his temper, he threw his knife at one of the stones. As if in slow motion, a small spray of sparks erupted as the knife glanced off the rock, stunning them both.

"Did you see that?" said Fingland.

"I sure did!" answered Jamie as he sank to his knees to examine the stone in the gathering dusk. Jamie could see two distinct layers of color. The side he had tried at first was red with a speckled texture, but the side his knife had hit was smooth and dull grey.

Then he looked around for his knife. All he could see was a tangle of vines. Putting the rock down, he started feeling around for his knife with both hands. He'd already learned it would be key to their survival, so how could he have thrown it away? "How childish can I be?" he mumbled to himself. With a growing feeling of panic threatening to overwhelm him, Jamie continued to probe the tangled surface growth. Just then, he felt the handle and pulled it free from the vines. Except for a scuffing on the side, it appeared undamaged. "No worries, Dad," he exclaimed. "I found it!"

But now he had to try again to create a spark. This time, he would be patient and methodical. Cradling the rock in his left hand, Jamie positioned it above the tinder. In one smooth stroke he brought the back of his knife down on the grey stone. Several sparks flashed down, but failed to land where he wanted. It took four tries before Jamie coaxed a spiral of smoke from a handful of fluff brush. By full dark a cheery fire was warming their cold hands.

Fingland pulled a space blanket out of his carry bag. "What are these things for?" he asked.

"I don't really know, they were in the survival kit. They seemed so thin and there was no climate control on them."

"What did the manual tell you?"

Jamie looked at his father from under his brow, "You mean the auto-manual, the one that doesn't work anymore?"

"Sorry, I'm embarrassed I asked."

Jamie just shrugged, pulling his space blanket out too. "Dad, maybe we could use these to make another lean-to, if we tie these two together with neuro-fiber and cut some branches to hold the ends up."

It turned out that neither one of them was very good at tying knots, but after a while they did get the two blankets to stay together. Cutting small branches by firelight was also challenging but soon they had a crude lean-to sitting by the fire. The stripped branches had yielded a pile of silver-green leaves, making their first mattress in the wild. Sitting cross-legged, Jamie began to relax. Fingland was too stiff to sit like his son, so he lay on his side, his face aglow from the small blaze. In silence, they munched on survival wafers and Herman nuts.

*Alheeza crept to within sight of their fire and then crawled a little closer. He shook involuntarily as images of the attack came back to him. A deep feeling of loss and fatigue engulfed him. His head swam as he eased himself into the woolly surface growth.*

*Through heavy lidded eyes, he watched the creatures assemble their structure. It still amazed him, the way they could put things together. If his kind could just do that!*

*His stomach growled, reminding him that he'd had nothing to eat that day.*

---

After they had settled in the lean-too and Jamie had eaten his fill, he looked out toward the glade from which they'd emerged earlier that evening. Suddenly, he felt another wave of hunger, almost as if his stomach growled but it had not. He looked again and noticed two points of yellow light. It was almost like that creature was following them. The more he stared, the more he was sure he too was being watched. Then the wave of hunger hit again. Where was that coming from?

On impulse he reached into his sleeping sleeve, pulling out a handful of Herman nuts. Instead of taking a bite, he flung them into the darkness toward the yellow eyes. It seemed to duck away but in a few moments, it was back.

---

*The alien had thrown something at him, as if it knew exactly where he lay in the surface growth. At first he had ducked away, but then he heard the light patter of something land behind him. Fear welled up at first, but then he caught a whiff of freshly shelled nuts. He crept slowly forward. There was no mistaking it, there before him was one of his favorite foods. Had the creature somehow known he was hungry? No! That just could not be!*

---

Jamie was pretty sure that the creature was eating the nuts he had thrown and the funny thing was that his feeling of hunger had passed.

# The Precipice

---

*A*lheeza thought back to when the creatures had crashed into the forest, it was seven sun cycles. For the last three, he had followed them, making sure to stay well back and out of sight. They seemed to pick the same type of areas to spend each night. There had not been another Great Raptor sighting since that terrible night. He did his best to stay hidden after dark, but still as close to the aliens' fire as possible.

If they continued in this northerly direction, they would reach the Snarling River by midmorning.

---

The faded orange swamp bellower trumpeted his challenge to all comers. The ground shook as he pawed the turf with an immense three-toed foot, throwing rocks and dirt into the air. He swung his massive head from side to side, and from under a palisade of irregular horns, he searched the valley with his small eyes. His immense chest swelled as he drew in their scent through his narrow-brow nostrils and bellowed his challenge again. With mating season raging within him, any fight would do.

Fingland and Jamie stood almost a kilometer from the hill, but they could clearly see the huge animal blocking their way.

Fingland spoke first, "Would you look at the size of that one!"

"We won't be going over that hill any time soon, that's for sure!" replied Jamie. He went on, "Let's track around to the east of it and then head north again. That looks like an opening between the hills over there."

As they turned to go, a challenge could be heard off to the west. The trumpeting echoed through the hills as they made their way into the mottled forest. Pushing past tangled red leaved bushes, they came upon a ravine with a little stream tumbling over a bed of round stones. One side was thick with the rosy underbrush but the other was fairly open, making it easier for them to find their way. It looked as if it would take them safely past the raging animal on the high ground whose grunting and bellowing grew distant as they picked their way down the gully.

Sometime later, Jamie thought he could hear rushing water ahead. On impulse, he climbed the ravine pushing through the underbrush, and breaking out into the open. Before him was a ledge covered with the familiar twisted ground cover. He caught his breath at what lay beyond. From this vantage point, a vast valley stretched out before him, filled with purple and lime-green trees. Carefully, he stepped towards the ledge that turned out to be a sizable cliff overhanging a raging river. A sense of foreboding made him step back from the precipice. Looking out at the panorama beyond, he was spellbound by the sight of the mountains, which stood above a distant plateau. Standing waves of an angry river rushed into the steep bend below, apparently cutting away at the hill they were standing on. He had seen all of this from the survey skimmer, but looking down from the cliff he wondered how they would ever cross such a formidable barrier. It had seemed like weeks ago that they had flown over it, but only seven days had passed since the fateful crash. Jamie reached up to touch his dead implant, regretting its loss once again.

Fingland burst through the underbrush, where he stood for a moment taking in the view. He strode past Jamie to stand on the very edge of the precipice, where he looked at the panorama saying, "Oh, isn't this magnificent!" Pointing, he continued, "Base Camp is just over those mountains."

"That's just what I was thinking."

Turning back to look at Jamie, Fingland said, "I think we really can do this, I mean walking back to Base Camp, your mother, and civilization. I'm starting to feel like my old self again, and I know in my heart we can do this together."

A smile started to spread across Jamie's face as he looked at his father. Finally, he seemed more like his old self again. He was looking across the ravine toward the distant mountains when he heard a dull thump. One moment Jamie was staring at his father and the next he simply vanished.

"Dad!" Jamie screamed as he dropped to his knees looking over the freshly scarred edge of the cliff, catching a glimpse of his father atop a wedge of soil as it exploded upon impact with a protruding rock. Like a rag doll, Fingland flailed downward until he was swallowed up by the standing waves of the raging river. Jamie stopped breathing as he watched wide-eyed as the scene unfolded. Then he caught sight of something downstream. Could it have been his father? Could he have survived such a terrible fall?

He sat back stunned. For the second time in just a few days he was all alone in a strange world. Tears welled up and his throat tightened as he remembered the harsh words he had spoken to his father in the last days. Silently, the tears started sliding down his cheeks.

# Strange Bed Fellows

*A**lheeza had seen the larger one of the pair drop out of sight when the cliff gave way. Again he was filled with the sense of death and loss. Where were these feelings coming from?*

*He watched the remaining one, sitting silently at the edge of the cliff. Much of the afternoon passed, and still it did not move. Would it make a fire soon, because there were more dangers in the woods than just the Great Raptors? He could not wait too long, or he would have to find his own shelter with darkness so close. There was the special place along the stream bed.*

"Dad, I'm so sorry, I didn't mean to get so angry," Jamie mumbled to himself. "How could you leave me like this?"

He felt numb with grief as he stared out at the mountains where only an amber glow was left from the setting sun. Before him, the valley had been turned into an undulating ocean of frozen grey waves, the details of the forest lost in the twilight.

"You were just standing there and then whoosh, you were gone."

Jamie staggered to his feet, slowly slinging his bag over his shoulder. He stood like that for a few moments, gazing about like a bewildered drunk.

"Where to now?" he muttered to himself.

Then that feeling of premonition came over him again. It was as if an image flashed in his head, revealing a snug place to take cover for the night. He made his way back towards the stream, clambering down to follow its narrow ravine as it dropped towards the river.

*Curled up on a ledge near the back of the cave, Alheeza was settling in for a safe night's sleep when he heard scraping coming from outside. To his horror, the alien was scrambling up the slope that led to the cave, cut deeply into the soft bank. It stopped when it sensed him lying there.*

―――――――○――――――――

Jamie could see a pair of eyes reflecting the dim evening light. He froze in place, not sure what was hiding there. He stepped back reflexively holding his hands in front of him, palms out.

―――――――○――――――――

*There it was making those same gestures again. He knew from watching that it was a clever creature, but what to do next? The alien seemed anxious as it strained to see into the cave. Slowly he moved out of the dark shadows, coming out just enough to reveal himself.*

―――――――○――――――――

A wave of relief washed over Jamie as he saw that it was the familiar animal from the glade. "Oh, it is you again my little friend. You scared the crap out of me." Jamie said more to himself than the creature. "Did you find yourself a nice place to hold up for the night?"

―――――――○――――――――

*More of its strange utterances, but there was no threat there.*

*They stood staring at each other as the last of the light faded. Glancing up a shadow cut through the star field far above, followed by the scream of a distant Raptor. That sent them both scrambling into the cave. Alheeza's night vision still let him see the strange creature as it fumbled about feeling for a level place to settle. It came to rest on the far side of the little cave, pulling its bag of things close.*

*He sensed a fear and fatigue mixed with grief that was almost paralyzing. These things must be coming from the alien, but how? Soundless speech was not a gift of the lesser creatures. Now he found himself sharing his hide-away with this strange being. Oddly enough, he felt less alone.*

Jamie could not remember ever feeling so tired. He was on the edge of tears but he drove himself to feel around in his bag, pulling out one of his dirty jump-suits. Once he was dressed in several layers and wrapped in his space blanket, he felt a little better. The fact that he was sharing a cave with an alien creature did not seem to bother him, in fact there was some sort of comfort in its presence. He started to think back to the screams he had heard outside, and how instinctively he had feared for his life.

He pulled out some Herman nuts and tried eating, but he was too upset to continue. Instead he reached out, towards the creature, dropping the morsel on the ground. Then he curled into a ball wrapping the thin blanket tightly about his head. He wept quietly, reliving the horror of seeing his father swept away from him. His harsh words with his father made him feel even worse. The man who meant everything to him was gone and he was totally alone, except for a strange being from this unworldly planet.

Sleep finally took him and he dreamed fitfully: *I would not eat that cluster of white berries if I was you, said his companion. Our race learned long ago what was poisonous. 'But they looked and smelled so good', he heard himself say, but there was something strange in the way they spoke and everything seemed disjointed. Come, said his companion, and Jamie dropped the berries to follow.*

Jamie awoke in the dark, the dream still clinging to him into his wakefulness. He lay as still as possible listening. Yes, there was a steady intake of breath not that far from him. What had woken them? Then he heard it, something caused a stone to shift outside followed by a sharp intake of breath next to him. He waited, holding his breath, and then it came again. Jamie tensed, straining to hear more. He looked out towards the cave mouth and found that the faint moonlight illuminated the stream bed enough that he could make out simple details. What was out there? A feeling of dread crept over him.

Time seemed to stand still as he drew measured breaths. Without knowing how, his hand found his trusty knife. By feel, he unfolded the largest blade. Gripping it tightly, he strained to hear what was coming.

*Alheeza awoke with a start, fear tingling through his body. The acrid scent of the approaching wilda-cat brought him to full alert. How had he been so careless as to not heed the faint traces over the past days? Now he was cornered without a family unit for protection.*

A sliver of moon was just enough for Jamie to make out a squat creature edging along the gully, head low, snuffling as it came. It was hard to tell how big it was. It had an odd gait with tall hind legs, shorter front legs set on either side of a broad chest, and bristling shoulder spines. It turned its blunt snout toward the cave opening, its luminous eyes probing inside.

Jamie felt an electric jolt of fear stab down his spine. He sensed his cave partner moving to face the threat. Slowly his raised his knife and took a deep breath. The approaching creature hesitated.

Without knowing why, he felt himself launch forwards screaming loudly. It was overlapped by his companion's high pitched screech as it leapt beside him.

They landed just in front of the intruder as Jamie's knife slashing down, narrowly missing its head as it twisted and leaped back. Gravel sprayed up from the stream bed as the predator raced away from them.

Jamie stood breathing heavily, as he watched the dark creature disappear into the shadows. Beside him, the glade creature panted deeply.

*What had just happened? Alheeza had planned to attack the wilda-cat but that was a desperate move against a dangerous adversary. How had the alien known to attack at the very same moment, making their combined strength a deciding factor? As he was weighing these factors he turned to look up at the alien. Their eyes met and for an instant there was a feeling of oneness.*

Jamie did not know much about the animals on this planet but one thing was clear, this little creature with the big eyes was somehow his friend and ally, but how?

As he puzzled over this, his companion turned and went back into the cave. Given the chill of the night, he shrugged and followed it back into the protection of the overhang.

# Charlie and Me

When he awoke, stiff and cold, the cave was empty. Jamie made his way back to where his father had fallen the day before. He sat in the woolly turf gazing at the shredded cliff edge. He somehow sensed the approach of the glade creature but kept his eyes fixed on the gorge where his father had vanished. His throat was tight with grief, and the paralysis of indecision was taking hold again.

"What am I going to do? I miss you so much, Dad!" Jamie muttered as tears started to fall again. "It's all my fault, maybe we should have stayed by the skimmer."

He reached behind his ear, whispering, "Symone what should I do?" There was nothing but silence. He dropped his hand and wept some more.

He sat there for the longest time, and then he looked up to the distant mountain in the north. Could he make it on his own to Base Camp and his mother? He doubted that very much.

He turned to meet the glade creature's unblinking green eyes. "What do you think I should do?"

*It kept making those odd noises from time to time. As he studied the alien, he became more convinced that it was suffering from grief at the loss of its older partner. His own loss of the genetic elders made him feel alone as well. Was there a parallel link here? It kept staring off into the north as if longing to go there. Odd, since that was where he planned to join his race at the gathering place.*

*If he was going to reach the crossing, it was time to get moving.*

*Other denzels would be arriving early, and he was eager to rejoin his community. Getting to his feet, Alheeza padded off at an easy pace. After a moment, he heard the alien follow.*

As if in a dream, Jamie got to his feet, shouldering his bag, and then he followed the creature towards the woods and the highlands beyond.

*The sun was climbing well into the sky when Alheeza saw the mist hanging above the trees ahead. While they traveled towards it, a distant rumbling grew in intensity until it was a resounding roar. Breaking through the underbrush, the entire Snarling River cascaded over a rocky shelf where it crashed far below, raising a column of mist that obscured the valley beyond.*

*Alheeza turned to look upstream, where the full volume of the Snarling River gushed from a slot in the rock cliff beyond. Somewhere up there in the palisade of flat tipped conifers, was a tree bridge and Alheeza hoped it was still in place.*

Jamie had never imagined standing on a precipice, where the rocks seemed to vibrate from the roar of the waterfall. The river came boiling out of a narrow slot in the rocky hill above, before it plunged over the ledge to the depths below. The raging river seemed like an impenetrable barrier.

When he turned, his companion was picking his way up the rocky slope.

"I am going to have to find a name for you my little friend," Jamie said, falling in behind.

With the roar of the falls behind him, Jamie climbed towards the tall flat-topped conifers along the crest of the hill. As he panted up the slope, the strange animal ahead did not seem to tire with the ascent. To his surprise, it paused as if knowing Jamie needed to catch his breath. Climbing on, they came to a palisade of tall trees. Beyond the giant hedge, they broke out onto another ledge.

In awe, Jamie looked about, mist from the gorge rose until it dripped from everything. Far below, the entire river was crashing through a narrow stone canyon. It did not shake and roar like the water fall, but it still was an impressive barrier. Bridging the span was an uprooted conifer, its bushy branches long devoid of their foliage. The glistening wet trunk sagged from its own weight. The creature stepped onto it and looked back at him, as if to say, "This way."

As Jamie looked down he muttered, "Oh yeah! Just step onto the tree and walk across. Don't mind the 100 meter drop!"

Gripping a branch, he experimentally took a step onto the wet tree. His foot slipped and he almost fell but was able to grab another branch just in time.

"Oh, crap!" he exclaimed as he struggled to regain his balance.

Breathing heavily, he stared down into the boiling water. "Right, just one wrong step and I'm a dead man!"

---

*About one third of the way across, Alheeza turned to see if the alien followed. He saw it slip, just catching itself before plummeting into the gorge. He had expected it to be more sure footed, after all he had no trouble climbing trees.*

*As he watched, it slipped its foot skin off, experimentally testing its traction on the tree trunk. Then it removed the other foot skin and stuffed it in its bag. Looking wide-eyed, it tried to mount the wet log again, cautiously working its way towards him.*

---

Jamie was shaking from the near fall. He had removed his foot wear for it had no traction on the wet surface. With bare feet, he now could feel the roughness under the glistening surface. Carefully he stepped onto the sagging tree taking a cautious step while holding onto a branch. It seemed better, so he tentatively reached for the next branch and edged past it. All was going well until he looked down. The swirling rapids below seemed to make his world spin and he almost lost his grip. In his head he heard: *keep your eyes on me.* In that moment he looked up to see the unblinking green eyes of the glade creature staring back at him.

"I can do this!" Jamie said to himself. "I can do this!" Fixing his gaze on the creature, he took halting steps towards the other side. Twice he felt his foot slide, but his firm grip on the interspersed branches kept him upright.

His companion was waiting for him on the other side.

"Can you believe that!" he exclaimed. "I'll bet nobody from the ship would believe I've just crossed that thing!" He squatted to eye level with his companion, "I think there is far more to you than meets the eye, my little friend. You're no dummy, are you? What am I going to call you? They looked at each other and then Jamie said, "How would you like Charlie?" and then pointing to himself he said, "I'm Jamie!"

───────────⊂⊃───────────

*All of this chatter was a little distracting, but Alheeza was getting the distinct impression that the alien was very excited about the tree bridge. It kept pointing at him and repeating the same noises. What was this about? The funny thing was that he was starting to hear patterns in its chattering. "Charlie" was repeated clearly. Then he noticed that it was pointing to itself repeating "Jamie." Then it hit him, it was introducing itself to him.*

───────────⊂⊃───────────

Charlie, as he now thought of him, seemed to bow, or at least nodded his head. Then he turned and padded off down a narrow trail through the trees towards the valley below.

# The Crystal

*A*lheeza worked his way down the rocky cliff with Jamie following behind. Once clear of the tall trees, they descended down the rocky ledges, passing through thick bushes with long drooping yellow leaves. Soon they found themselves standing on the upper ledge of a descending set of steaming pools, fed by a steaming rivulet gurgling out of a layered shiny yellow mound.

*Padding carefully along the edge, he tested the temperature of the first pool with his forepaw. Then without hesitation he descended to the third pool, where he found it more to his liking. Slipping into the hot water he splayed out his legs and let his body float into the middle of the pool. All his scales released allowing the healing warmth to penetrate his being. It was the first time since the taking of his elders, that Alheeza felt completely relaxed.*

It was the most unusual thing he had ever seen. Jamie had followed Charlie down past the steaming pools that formed at each terrace of glistening stone, but he was not prepared for what happened next. The little fellow simple walked straight into the pungent smelling water. The wisps of vapor enveloped his body. All that could be seen of him was the top of his head with his brow nostrils, relaxed ears and closed eyes. The partially exposed shoulder showed a surprising array of bristling tiny plates.

He watched for a while and slowly became aware of his own deep fatigue and aching muscles. Tentatively, he reached a hand towards the edge of the pool and found it very warm, if not a bit hot. Looking around he muttered to himself, "I haven't felt warm water since Base Camp. What the heck!"

His jump-suit, under trousers and shoes made a neat pile as his carefully stepped into the water. "Oh, that feels nice!" he said as he edged into the steaming water. Sitting with just his head out, he felt the pain of his ordeal easing.

---

*Alheeza's eyes were partially immersed when he became aware of animated activity at the edge of the pool. The alien had stepped out of its wrinkled outer skin. He watched in fascination, not having had a good look close up before. It shed a smaller skin from around its midsection and to his amazement it had a small nose with a pouch at its middle section, as well as a small tuft of the same filaments as its head covering. Soon it ambled to the edge and came into his pool.*

---

How long Jamie basked in the pungent bath, he could not tell, but a feeling of light headedness brought him crawling to the edge. In the afternoon sun, he quickly dried.

It was some time later that his companion stepped from the water, his small scales closing as the water dripped from his body. He gazed at Jamie for a moment and then padded off down the trail leading to the valley. Jamie was following, but as they passed the last pool, he thought he could hear music. Well not exactly music but there was a rhythmic humming that seemed to come from a jumble of broken rock. Casting his eye over the tumbled stone, he could make out a cluster of rocky nodes that seemed to have been shattered from some previous disturbance. It looked a bit like a cluster of stony eggs and several had been broken open. One of the shattered orbs caught his attention. As he stepped closer, he could see something red gleaming from within its white crystalline interior. The un-earthly music became more intense as he drew near.

Jamie could feel his excitement rising as he looked about for a way to open the cracked node. Poking about he found another cracked orb and on impulse he picked up a loose rock and smashed it down, breaking it open. A slender amber crystal was trapped within its white-jewelled interior. He pried it out where he admired its beauty in the sun. Slipping it into his pouch he set about hammering the first node with the stone. After knocking another section away, he was able to retrieve the finger long ruby crystal. As he held it aloft, the sun caught its smooth facets making it gleam. He could almost feel the strange rhythms coming from within.

"What a beautiful stone!" he said to himself.

While Jamie clutched the red crystal, the music faded. He looked around at a world that had taken on a new vibrancy. He heard his companion returning, so he turned and what he saw made his breath stop, because the creature that he called Charlie, now shimmered. Was he hallucinating?

*What did you find?* came a question into his head. It was not like the words especially, it was more like a thought.

*You really are the most peculiar creature, the way you can pick things up.* Came another thought in his head and then: *That is a very interesting stone you are holding.*

Jamie spun around, looking to see if someone was talking to him. He was going crazy, hearing imaginary things.

*What is the matter with you? We need to get down this hill and find a safe place before nightfall. One of your fires would be a very welcome thing, especially with Great Raptors about.*

Jamie looked back at Charlie, still clutching his red crystal and said, "Am I going crazy, I can hear voices in my head? Can you hear them too?"

This time the creature jumped as if shocked. Again Jamie heard a voice in his head: *What voices?*

*A strange voice in my head!* Jamie thought.

The creature looked stunned. *This cannot be. It is only our race that can communicate with mind-speak,* heard Jamie in his head.

*Mind-speak, what's that?* Jamie thought.

*Mind-speak is the way our race communicates. How can you be doing it too?*

*Oh crap! I am going crazy. Now I think it's talking to me!* Jamie spun around as if to run back up the hill but within his head he heard a plea.

*Do not go, for I understand you! I should not be able to understand you, but you speak to me as if you are one of our kind. I do not know how this is possible, but I understand you.*

Jamie looked back at Charlie in disbelief thinking, *You can understand me?*

*Yes!*

*Am I crazy? Here I am standing here in front of this four legged creature, thinking that I am telepathically communicating with it.*

*I am not an "it", and my name is Alheeza, not the "Charlie" you keep saying in gibberish. I am a denzel and this is my home. I am pretty sure this has never been your home.*

Involuntarily Jamie sat down, staring into his companion's unblinking green eyes.

*You're not an it, and your name is Alheeza. A denzel!* Jamie mind-spoke, not quite sure how this mind-speaking was controlled.

Jamie looked down at the ruby crystal in his hand, and then back up at his shimmering companion. The intelligence and compassion in those eyes could not be his imagination.

Fingering the stone, he mind-spoke: *Could it be the crystal? Could it have opened something between us? I felt something before, something I could not explain. I had sudden feelings that I had to act upon, but when I picked up this red stone, my whole world changed. I could see you in different colors and hear your thoughts.*

*You look the same to me, but I hear your thoughts, and quite frankly, I am surprised at how intelligent you seem.*

Clutching the stone to his chest Jamie took a deep breath and went on: *I have to say the same. I thought you were just a clever alien dog.*

*What is a dog?*

*Never mind that. It wasn't a coincidence, was it? I found water and food because you were there showing me the way.*

*I have suspected that I was feeling your emotions, but did not want to believe it possible. For me, I grew thirsty and you followed. I grew hungry and you followed, and my suspicions grew. Now here we are mind-speaking. Perhaps it is the crystal, I do not know, but you are speaking in the manner of my kind, and I understand you perfectly well.*

Jamie just stared at him open-mouthed.

*What are you known as?* Alheeza wondered.

"Jamie," is all he said, and then, in mind-speak: *My family call me Jamie, but my adult name will be Jamblyn Chambers. And yes, I am not from around here. This might be hard to understand, but we came from a great distance across the stars and this is the first planet I have ever walked upon.*

*Many questions, but let me ask this first, how could you travel across the stars?*

Not sure how to proceed, Jamie went on: *I knew this was going to be difficult. Technology is how we came here.*

*That makes no sense to me.*

*Let me try again. Our people, our race of beings, have learned over time to change things around us. We learned to make fire, tools and, after thousands of years of learning, we made a thing that would carry many of us through the stars to visit a new place. Your planet was a new hope for us.*

*The fire I understand and I saw you come in a flying thing. Is this thing something you call technology?*

*Yes, that is it exactly! We had many things that worked for us, but the day we crashed was the day all of our technology failed. To make it simple, I have no way to travel across the stars anymore. We have lost all of our smart tools and now I just have my hands, wits, and this small knife.*

*Yes, I have seen you use it to cut things and make fire. That still impresses me very much, for none of our race can conjure up fire from nothing. We fear fire, but somehow I sense that fire in your hands is safe.*

*Well safe is a relative term, but yes I can make a fire and so far have contained it.*

Alheeza just stood staring at him, making Jamie nervous.

Finally the slim denzel mind-spoke: *Although you speak in my head, in the manner of my kind, there are things that you say that make no sense to me. We will have to discuss this later, for it is very important for me to understand you better. For now I greet you, Jamie, also known as Jamblyn Chambers, from the stars. Night will come with its many dangers, especially the Great Raptors. One of your fires would be most welcome.*

# Pursued from Above

Jamie slipped the precious stone into his belt along with the amber one, and as he did so, his world dulled fractionally. "This is all so bizarre!" he muttered to himself. Then he realized he couldn't sense his companion's thoughts anymore. Overcome by a feeling of emptiness, he took out the light-coloured crystal gripping it firmly. Some enhanced senses returned, but not with full intensity. Quickly, he exchanged the stones, holding the ruby colored stone once again. The emptiness vanished as he followed his new companion down the trail.

As his guide padded ahead of him, Alheeza mind-spoke: *Now I know why you make those noises, it is your kind of communication, is it not?*

"Yes!" Jamie said, hurrying after him. There was no further conversation for an hour or so but finally Jamie broke the mental silence between them: *Can you read my mind, my every thought?*

Alheeza replied in his silent way: *That is not how it works with our race. We project what we want to be understood. We share a concept. How we get to those thoughts, is a private matter. When I think back to the glade when I was watching you, I had the impression I was getting feelings from you. I tried to ignore it but I am sure there was some rudimentary connection after your flying thing hit the ground.*

*Yes, the crash, a lot of things have been different since the crash,* mind-spoke Jamie, shaking his head.

Jamie following Alheeza as he worked his way through the forest in the valley.

*What do we need for protection tonight, in case the Raptors come again?* asked Jamie in mind-speak.

*Our kind prefer caves or clusters of heavy overgrowth. Much was taught to me by my genetic elders, but I am very inexperienced by our races' standard, being just 17 season cycles of age.*

*We're almost the same age, you and me!* mind-spoke Jamie. Then he added: *For our shelter tonight would one of those Herman nut groves work? Those tangled heavy branches must be like a tree fortress against a large flying creature?*

*Yes, that was where I was headed. May I ask, how is it that you can make fire without fear?*

*Oh that is pretty new to me too, but I read about it my book.*

*Book, what is that?*

*I'll show you tonight.*

---

Not long before sunset, they found a large Herman nut grove. The twisted interlocking branches came all the way down to the ground and they had to pick their way carefully to enter the open area within. The thick canopy of purple leaves made it very dark inside and Jamie took advantage of the fading light to gather as much fire wood as possible. Alheeza even got into it by dragging dry branches from the base of adjacent trunks. Jamie prepared to start a fire, with an area scraped clear at the base of a wide twisted tree trunk. Using some dry fluff brush fibre as the starting tinder, he struck sparks off his stone by using the back of his knife. It took several tries, but finally a spiral of smoke, carefully blown upon, turned into an orange flame.

Alheeza sat amazed at what he was seeing. He mind-spoke: *This is unbelievable, sitting here watching you making a fire out of nothing.*

*It's all in this book,* telepathed Jamie as he reached into his pack drawing out Tom Brown's Field Guide to Wilderness Survival. He flipped open a page that showed how to use his knife to make sparks by hitting it against a chunk of flint. His alien friend looked down at the open pages with interest.

*It does not speak in my head. I see squiggles and marks but nothing speaks to me. How does this work?*

*Oh, it's a book. I read the words and the illustrations show me how something should look.*

*What is "read the words?"*

Using his finger to point out he words, Jamie read from page 77, "Striking the Spark. Make a large tinder bundle, line it with very soft material, and place it on a piece of dried bark. Then hold the rock just above the tinder, strike a sharp edge of it with the back of your knife blade until a spark falls onto the tinder."

*You pull those words from this thing? Now that is magic.*

*No, it's just reading. All kids learn to read from age five,* mind-spoke Jamie.

*Remarkable!*

They sat there for some time in silence. Finally, Alheeza mind-spoke: *Try to tell me where you came from.*

Jamie threw more fuel on their crackling fire before answering. *We came from across the stars. As you may have surmised, we were not just from across the sea, but from a world much like this that orbited around a star far away.*

*That seems impossible?*

*Let me ask, do you know that you live on a vast orb that revolves around your sun, just like your moons go around your planet?*

*My genetic elders were part of the group of observers who believed we were small creatures living on an immense orb. Your story supports their belief and that makes it easier to believe. Now tell me something about the place you came from.*

*We called it Earth. It is so far away that you cannot imagine being able to travel to it. In fact, I have never seen it. I was born onboard our interstellar space craft, about one year after my parents fled Earth. This is the first time I have lived in a forest and seen all the marvels that you take for granted.*

Alheeza just blinked at him for a while. Finally he telepathed: *You have never set foot on solid ground until recently? You grew up somewhere between the stars? This is all very strange, but what I do understand is that your race had a type of magic we could never have had, and you are here now. Somehow, I believe my survival is now tied to yours and vice versa. More understanding than that may not be needed for now.*

Jamie looked down at the crystal and then back up to his new-world friend. He mind-spoke: *There was a magic here as well, not everything is easily explained.*

Before settling in to sleep next to the fire, Jamie took a closure cord from his sleeping sleeve and fashioned a crude cradle to sling the ruby crystal about his neck. As it rested against his skin, he felt the connection with this planet.

---

Jamie was startled awake. Not knowing what had woken him, he took inventory. He was curled on his side; his limbs were chilled despite his layered clothing. All he could see was the glow of a few coals from their evening fire. His only real comfort came from warmth along his back. Reaching around he felt a warm Alheeza pressed against him. It felt kind of nice and then he heard it, deep wing beats far above. He held his breath.

Alheeza stirred behind him. *A Great Raptor!*

From the sound, it must be circling high above, thought Jamie. As he listened the sound grew closer until their world thundered from its approaching wing strokes. The tree shuddered as the creature landed in the canopy above. A paralyzing terror swept through Jamie as his nostrils filled with a stench of something long rotted.

As if reading his mind, Alheeza mind-spoke: *It's the Great Raptor that emits that horrible smell.*

In the dark, things started to crash down about them. Jamie did not know why he reached into his jump-suit to pull out the amber-coloured stone. Instantly, it transformed the black night into shadowed detail. All about them the air was thick with shredded leaves and bits of falling wood, but worse yet he could make out the stinking creature's head as it tore at the canopy above. Drawing courage from within, he reached out with a shaking hand to pluck a few small bits of kindling from his stash.

*You can do it,* mind-spoke Alheeza.

Coming to his knees he carefully placed several bits on the hot coals and blew gently.

The Great Raptor's scream cut through the night, making him jump, but somehow he was able to blow one more time on the coals. A small flame leapt up to lick the kindling. More debris rained down around them as the giant night killer thrashed about trying to pierce through the thickly-tangled branches.

As the fire flared, it lit the tree base. He added more fuel and the fire leapt higher. Jamie stood and not knowing why, he held the red crystal high. Whether it was the reflected light of their fire or some unknown inner flame, the stone burst forth with a startling ruby brilliance.

Far above he could see the Great Raptor squinting at him. It let out another deafening scream before its wings thundered, lifting it into the night sky. Where the creature had once been, stars twinkled through the shredded canopy.

*How did you do that?* asked Alheeza.

*Do what?*

*Make that crystal come alive.*

*I don't know!* mind-spoke Jamie, as he looked down at his shaking left hand that still clutched the precious stone.

---

When morning came, its first light stabbed through the shattered canopy above. Broken branches hung from tattered strips of bark. It was only the thicker branches that had held the Raptor at bay. For Jamie it was sobering to see how close the predator had come to penetrating their tangled fortress.

*My race live long and pass their memories to the next generation. Although my training is not complete, I have no memory of a stone that possess powers like yours,* mind-spoke Alheeza.

Jamie was sitting cross-legged with his back against the mighty tree, still holding his crystal. As he looked down at it, he mind-spoke: *I have no idea how this stone works or what properties it really has. Everything that has happened to me has been like walking in a dream.*

---

They had been making their way through dense forest for hours, with little or no communication between them. It was hard to tell when he became aware of the sound of running water ahead. *What is that sound?* he mind-spoke.

*It is the great Snarling River again; we crossed it by way of the log bridge, before you learned to speak.*

Jamie followed Alheeza as he wove his way through the low brush that formed the ground cover within the tall forest. When they broke out into the open, he could not have been more surprised. Before him was a slow moving muddy river, about 300 meters across. The river banks were low and the overhanging trees formed a shaded path as it worked its way north. They followed it for most of the afternoon, but at a bend in the river, Jamie noticed an unexpected spot of color along the stony shoreline. Something was snagged on an exposed root. A chill ran down Jamie's spine as he realized what he was looking at.

---

*Alheeza watched as the young alien jumped down the bank, splashing his way through the shallow water. He stood on the bank watching, as Jamie threw himself on the broken body of his parent. The boy's face became wet, his shoulders heaved and a great wailing came from his mouth. Such a sorrowful sound he had never heard before. Somewhere deep in his racial memories came a similar wailing, and all of his feeling of loss came flooding back to him. Alheeza turned away, unable to look upon the grief-stricken alien any longer. The night of the attack came back to him, making his legs unsteady. How was it that he was having these strong feelings? It was not like his race to have repeated waves of emotion. They were taught to see the situation, evaluate it, take action, and file it in the ancestral memories. He thought he had done that. Was his training incomplete, was he going crazy, or was it the alien?*

---

How long Jamie clung to his dead father, he did not know. Finally he drew himself up, sniffing as he turned towards Alheeza.

Alheeza's words came into his head: *In what manner does your race honour its dead?*

*What are you talking about?*

*What do you want to do with your now-dead elder?*

Jamie was totally taken aback. He had never thought about what happened to the bodies of dead people. Back on Mayflower a few had died, but he did not know what happened to the body. It was just something he had never thought of. After a moment he mind-spoke: *How does your kind deal with a death?*

*Our race pass on the ancestral memories, the body is unimportant.*

Jamie looked down at the slack grey face of his father; the once bright eyes that gleamed with intelligence were dull. He swallowed past the lump in his throat, trying to think. Finally, he mind-spoke: *Help me, I do not know what to do.*

*Do you have ancestral memories tied to your parent?*

*Not like you do, but I have my memories of times we spent together. And there were the stories he told me of his life on Earth. So I guess I can say I have memories.*

*Then given the harshness of our land, and our need to find a safe place to spend the night, maybe it is best if we send him back along the river where his energy can be returned to our life stream.*

Jamie just stared down at his once-vibrant father, unable to move or speak.

*Did I offend you in some way?*

*No, I cannot say that you did. I just find it hard to make a move.*

*See the dark clouds where we came from?*

*Yes.*

*That will fill the river again before morning. The river will take him far away, reclaiming his energy. You must leave him so we can keep moving, because darkness comes bringing the night hunters with it.*

As if coming out of a dream, Jamie reached down to his father's cold left hand. The simple, unadorned silver ring, sat loosely on the shrivelled second finger. Jamie slipped it off, putting in on his own. Without ceremony, he took hold of his father's shoulders lifting him to free the snag. As he rolled him into the deeper current, Fingland's body started to drift downstream again. Tearfully, he watched as the man who had raised him, drifted away on the current. A few moments later, he mind-spoke: *OK, I can leave now.*

*Good, let us make haste.*

As he followed Alheeza over the bank and along the trail, he spun the ring with his thumb. It was all that he had from the time with his father. As he followed, his mind was back on the ship hearing laughter in his Dad's voice. Tears blurred the trail ahead.

---

The clouds Jamie had seen in the distance were now piling up around them, threatening rain. Again they found a Herman nut grove to shelter within. The rains came fast and furious after making camp. Sheltered under the large twisted trunk of the giant tree, they were dry enough. Jamie had even been able to make a small fire from the dried bark and leaves. In the glow of it, they started to communicate once again.

Uncharacteristically, it was Alheeza that started the discussion: *Today you mourned the loss of an important family member. Somehow in your presence, I feel things more than I am used to. I'm not sure how, but I feel we have become connected, that there is a tie between us I have not felt before. It is a mystery. Do you feel it too?*

*Yes, I feel it too and I know I would not have survived here without you. For that alone, I am very grateful. I feel overwhelmed with all of the new things, but I do not feel alone facing them now that you are my friend.*

Jamie thought to himself, that if the other young people from Mayflower could see him now, they would think he was completely crazy. Sitting here with a member of the denzel race on the planet Azimov-4, imagining that he could somehow communicate telepathically. As soon as the thought came, it passed, leaving him beside Alheeza, his new friend in an alien world.

They talked in their silent way well into the night, about the way of life in Alheeza's world. Morning found them curled together as the first bit of the sunlight penetrated the canopy.

While they walked together the next day, Alheeza continued to teach Jamie about the forest they traveled through. It was like seeing the forest for the first time. Little details about the smallest of the creatures became a marvel. It was the edible plants that were truly fascinating.

At one point, Jamie noticed a cluster of white berries and reached for them. Alheeza interrupted, telling him that they were poisonous. In that moment Jamie remembered the dream. *This all happened in a dream I had a few days ago, before we became friends. I remember it so clearly.*

# Seven Against Two

**D**eep in dense bush without visual references frustrated Jamie. He hadn't been able to see ahead since he last stood near the waterfall, but Alheeza seemed to know where they were going. Nevertheless, even he stopped from time to time, looking about before plunging forward. Soon they came upon an unusual tree that soared above all the rest. The purple serrated leaves made it stand out from the other plants, but it was the double twisted trunk that spiraled into the sky that was most amazing.

*This is the copeander tree,* Alheeza was saying in that mind-speak way they communicated. *It has many medicinal properties.*

*A copeander tree*, Jamie thought. This was another new concept. Somehow in his head, these new concepts were turned into words. It was like learning a new language instinctively. It seemed that it worked better when Alheeza was instructing him. When he had shown Alheeza the book, he had to explain it and then the concept was slowly assimilated. Jamie shrugged, and looked up into the multitude of branches that soared into the blue sky.

*I want to climb this one to see ahead.*

*Seeing ahead is always useful, if only my race could climb this kind of tree,* telepathed Alheeza. Then he added: *While you are up there, collect some of the red fruit. It is the season of ripening.*

The leafy giant had multiple small branches that radiated out from the spiraling twin trunks. Taking hold of the nearest branch, Jamie heaved himself up to start the 100 meter climb. In no time, he was panting from the exertion. By the time he reached the uppermost limbs, his arms and legs were screaming from fatigue. He clung to his perch catching his breath. The foliage was thin here and he had a good look around. To the north, the forest gave way to a steep set of hills and far beyond that stood the mountain range. It seemed no closer, despite two days of trekking. His heart sank as he estimated how much farther they had to walk. Then on the distant bluff something twinkled, like sunshine off a mirrored surface. Alheeza had shown him many marvels of the woods, but a sharply reflected object could only be man-made. For the first time since his father disappeared, his spirits soared at the thought of seeing another human being.

From the exertion of the climb, it was even harder to climb down. At the last moment, he remembered to collect some of the odd-looking fruit. Reaching the bottom he excitedly mind-spoke: *Alheeza, I think I see another ship on the hills several days to the north. Can you believe it? After days of walking in the wilderness, I might see some of my people again.*

*That appears to make you very happy. I look forward to being with my own race as well.*

*You are?* Jamie mind-spoke.

*Yes, but that is still far from here and our paths seem to be taking us in the same direction for now.*

---

That night they took refuge under the low-sweeping branches of an orange iron-wood tree. This was another of the forest giants, with a thick straight trunk and long branches that were weighed down with clusters of broad leaves. They made camp between two of the far reaching roots that stood above the ground.

They chose to stop early because clouds threatened rain again that night. Jamie pulled out his book, checking the section on shelters. By reading while clutching his crystal, Jamie was able to telepath enough information for Alheeza to grasp the basic concept. After discussing their options, they set about collecting the materials needed. Their shelter was made of a thatch of wide leaves, supported by branches laced together with bark strips.

Later that night they lounged by the small fire, savouring the multitude of fleshy fruits and meaty nuts. Jamie had been thumbing through his old book, sharing a section on wilderness weapons with his friend, when Alheeza stopped him.

*What is it?* Jamie asked in mind-speak.

*The smell of wilda-cat is heavy in the air tonight.*

*Is there more than one?*

*I cannot tell for sure, but there can be five or more in their hunting pack.*

Jamie thought for a moment and then asked: *How close are they?*

*They are still ranging wide of us.*

Jamie thought back to his book. Could he make a weapon using local materials? *Will the fire keep them away?* he telepathed.

*Yes, but only at night.*

*Then I have work to do my friend and you can help me. I need a strong straight branch, not too big around.*

---

Jamie had fallen into the habit of talking with himself. He was working a two-meter long branch from the iron-wood tree above them. "Just turn the sharpened end in the hot coals until it turns a light brown and the surface gets hard. Yeah, right but what do you do when the wood is orange to start with?"

He took it from the fire from time to time testing the tip of the stick. The core of the branch charred slowly, and bit by bit Jamie was able to shape the tip into a point. It was far from a razor sharp point, but the tapered point looked lethal.

"Hey! Alheeza look at this!" he said triumphantly.

*What am I to see?*

*See how the end of this is now pointed and hard?*

*Yes!*

On impulse, Jamie drove the shaft into the trunk of a nearby tree. It easily sank several centimeters into the living tree. As Jamie wrestled to free his spear he mind-spoke: *Did your race ever hunt and eat animals?*

*Oh yes, but that was many generations ago. The life force is strong in all living things, both plant and animal. We take only what we need to survive while honouring life around us.*

Jamie thought for a moment: *Didn't Tom Brown learn something like that from Stalking Wolf?*

*Yes, that impressed me! Your kind can learn from the forest too.*

*How much of a danger are the wilda-cats?*

*My foresight is only a probability, not a certainty!*

Jamie paused before answering: *I am starting to think your probabilities are more accurate than some of our certainties.*

Jamie thought that his Denzel companion seemed to smile, and he nodded back. The rain started not long after.

---

Jamie hoisted the bag over his shoulder and picked up the new iron-wood spear. He looked at their campsite one more time, smiling at the thatched lean-to that had kept them dry during the deluge.

Suddenly, he felt a wave of sadness, remembering the look in his father's eyes the moment before his fall. Would his father have been proud of him making a shelter in this foreign land? He would never know. If he could change anything, it would have been the harsh words before his father's death.

Alheeza's telepathed: *Is there something amiss?*

*No, I am coming!*

They kept going through the dense forest and in an hour or so they heard a distant yowling. Alheeza stopped, turned his head from side to side, sniffing the air.

*What?* Mind-spoke Jamie as he looked around trying to see movement.

*The wilda-cats are near. Stay vigilant!*

"Roger that!"

*What?*

*It means, yes.*

Not long afterwards, they broke out into an opening in the forest with a patch of blue sky framed by the interlaced trees. They had only made it part way across when Alheeza stopped them.

*Stand close, and watch the left side, I will watch the right.*

Instinctively, Jamie' hand pressed through his suit to give the crystal more contact with his skin. His senses seemed to enhance as he scanned his side of the clearing. Suddenly, he sensed movement in the brush! He felt Alheeza pressed against the back of his knees and a low rumble seemed to be coming from him.

Three of the creatures stepped into the clearing on Jamie's side. Grabbing the spear with both hands, he leveled the heavy weapon at the oncoming predators. *There are three on my side!* he mind-spoke.

*Four on mine.*

Jamie gritted his teeth crouching low over the spear. The biggest one lowered its head, stepping forward with its shoulder plates bristling. Its protruding jaw gaped open exposing irregular teeth that gleamed yellow in the sun. Jamie's fear was forgotten as the creature lunged straight at him. All he could do was lean forward, leveling his spear at the oncoming wilda-cat. Time seemed to slow as the cat charged directly at him. At the last moment Jamie flicked his spear up impaling the cat under the jaw. The shaft punched through the chest plates, burying itself deep within. Jamie was driven back by the impact. The creature let out a terrible scream, before slumping at his feet.

Behind him a high pitched shriek split the air, accompanied by guttural grunts. Jamie twisted his spear from the twitching body of his attacker and spun to the new threat. A bleeding Alheeza was on his hind legs fending off a large wilda-cat. Jamie leapt to the side and drove his spear into the second cat's shoulder. It reared up, twisting to bite at the embedded shaft. Jamie held on with all of his might as the snapping animal thrashed about. It staggered before falling onto its rump. It looked around in confusion as black-red blood bubbled from around the shaft. Jamie pulled his spear free and held it high to make a second thrust but Alheeza mind-spoke: *It is dying, step back with me.*

Jamie looked around but the other wilda-cats were keeping their distance.

*Step back very slowly and prepare in case one of them charges again!*

As they worked their way to the edge of the opening, the remaining hunters moved away from them. As if on some signal, they pounced on their fallen companions. Soon the glade was filled with snarling and grunts as the remaining wilda-cats tore at the bodies of their mates.

*They don't seem terribly upset about their friends' death!* Jamie mind-spoke.

*They are wilda-cats, they see no difference between friend and food!*

"Glad I don't have friends like that," muttered Jamie.

Still shaking from the encounter, Jamie turned to follow his companion. Alheeza had a torn ear and walked with a noticeable limp with dark blood oozing from his shoulder.

Jamie mind-spoke: *You're hurt; we should have a look at those wounds.*

*We must press on to find a safer place first.*

*But you are hurt. Let me see how bad it is.*

*No! It is not yet safe to stop. We must press on a little further.*

Reluctantly Jamie followed, but it was apparent that Alheeza was struggling to make progress and was soon panting. Reluctantly, he stopped and allowed Jamie to look him over. His torn right ear looked sore but not serious. It was the deep gash on his right shoulder that was causing all the pain.

Jamie asked in mind-speak: *How does your race treat injuries like these.*

*A member of our clan will lick sap from the copeander tree and then lick it back into our wound. I have no such member to apply the healing ointment.*

*You have me and we have the copeander fruit with us. I could try to apply that to your gash.*

Before Alheeza could complain, Jamie dug into his bag, coming up with two of their shrivelled red copeander fruit. Using his knife he cut it into strips, slipping one into his mouth. To his surprise, his tongue was hit with a sweet spiciness which numbed it. He chewed the flesh into a soft mush before spitting it into his hand. The tingling remained in his mouth as he rolled the pulp into a ball. Next, he gently pressed it into the open gash on Alheeza's shoulder. It was deeper than it looked, leaking a black-red blood that dripped down his smooth scales.

Jamie watched in fascination as the bleeding stopped. He then chewed up a smaller piece, applying that to his tattered ear. Alheeza seemed to relax as the wounds were tended.

*Does that feel better?* Jamie asked in their way of speech.

*Yes, that does feel a good deal better. Now we must press on, I want to distance ourselves from the marauding wilda-cats.*

*Me too!*

Alheeza's limp seemed improved as they pushed on through the forest. Not wanting to waste anything, Jamie popped the last section of the wrinkled red fruit into his mouth. The tingling went all the way down as he swallowed it and to his surprise he felt his energy returning.

*Hey Alheeza, you should eat some of this copeander as well!*

Without any further prompting, Alheeza accepted a portion of the fruit. When they continued, he appeared to step more lively.

---

In the early afternoon, they found another giant iron-wood tree. Its thick, tough branches came down to the ground, making a protective border against a possible Raptor attack. Jamie set about making camp for the night in the open space that surrounded the thick trunk.

Exhausted by his injuries, Alheeza curled into a ball falling instantly asleep.

In this horrific land, Jamie found that the best way to cope with his grief was to keep busy. He pulled out his old book and looked for further inspiration.

When Alheeza awoke after dark, his nostrils were filled with a sweet fragrance that seemed familiar but strange. Jamie was crouched by the fire with something steaming on the ground.

*What are you doing?*

*I am making us a stew for supper. How do you feel?* Jamie asked in mind-speak.

Alheeza started to stretch but stopped from the pain in his shoulder. *I came out better than our two attackers, but it will take more time to repair myself. I ask again, what are you doing? The longer we travel together the better I understand you, but supper and stew still do not mean anything.*

Jamie scooped out a portion onto a broad leaf, and set it steaming in front of his friend. *Let it cool and then taste it.*

He may not have understood the words supper and stew, but after the offered food cooled, Alheeza took to the warm nut and fruit concoction with real enthusiasm, smacking his lips noisily between bites.

Jamie wanted to let Alheeza sleep so he heaped fuel on their fire and dozed awhile. When he awoke from the evening chill, he built the fire back up and slept again. At one point he burst awake, hearing the distant scream of a Raptor, but that too died away and he dozed off again.

In the morning Alheeza was surprisingly agile. His recovery was truly remarkable; there was almost no limp to his stride.

Satisfied that his companion was on the mend, Jamie resumed scouring the hollowed-out limb that served as a hot rock stewing pot. While working, he looked down at his father's simple silver ring on his finger. Keeping busy had pushed the painful memories of his father's loss into the background, but now as he spun the ring with his finger, his stomach twisted as he recalled the last moments of seeing him alive.

*You miss him terribly.*

*I thought you couldn't mind read?*

*I do not need mind reading skills to see the distress you carry. If he was the kind of elder I had, he would have wanted you to carry on, live, and propagate for the survival of the race.*

*I don't think he would have used those words; nevertheless, they carry a bit of truth.*

*I feel much better today, thanks to your ministrations. I even think we will reach the hills today, yes?*

*Yes, I believe we will!*

Within the forest it had been almost impossible for Jamie to see the approaching bluff, but as they climbed the steep incline, its true height became clear. The tall trees gave way to shrubs, the exposed rocks impeding their progress. Stopping to catch his breath, Jamie looked back across the forested valley. The hills in the distance, where his father had fallen, seemed like a thin ridge from his vantage point. If this was any indication of scale, the mountains were still some distance away.

Alheeza mind-spoke: *We are almost at the top. We will be there before the sun reaches it full height.*

*Will it be warmer there?*

*During the day, yes.*

*Let us get on with it then.*

Jamie was puffing as they approached the crest of the hill. Looking back, it was like the view from their survey skimmer, with the forest spread out in an undulating flow of trees. They had made it all the way through that maze of dangers. A chill ran through him as he suddenly felt exposed, standing in the open. Where had that new fear come from?

At the crest of the hill, the plateau spread out before them. It was a gently rolling plain, mainly strewn with broken rock of varying sizes interspersed with patches of sand. Looking back he could see their foot prints in the finely ground rock.

It was Alheeza that drew Jamie's attention to the left. *See that object resting on the ridge, is that what you were looking for?*

Jamie squinted into the sunshine. Not far off along the ridge, the sun reflected off something shiny. It was the distinct shape of a survey skimmer, just like the one he and his father had flown in. His heart raced with the sudden excitement of seeing people again.

*It is best if you approach without me,* Alheeza mind-spoke. *I will take cover in the scrub bush over there where I can watch your progress.*

*That is a good idea,* Jamie mind-spoken.

Alheeza peered around the edge of his hiding place as he watched his alien friend walk toward the strange craft. He could see no movement of any kind.

# Amanda

A manda awoke from another tormented dream where a dark flying creature clawed at the skimmer, its fierce red eyes glaring at her through the canopy. From its massive mouth, its tongue lolled out over a double row of yellow teeth, drooling in anticipation of the kill.

As the dream disintegrated, her head still spinning, she looked through the smudged canopy. Was she still dreaming, or was someone walking towards her in the bright sunlight? Amanda blinked her gritty eyes trying to focus. Yes, a slender man was walking towards her. This must be a hallucination, she thought, because no one could be out here.

It was growing hot again in the cockpit of the skimmer. Amanda tried to swallow but her parched tongue only stuck to her palate.

Jamie was walking cautiously towards the lone skimmer. As he scanned the area, he sensed that something was wrong for the craft listed to one side, but there were no other signs of a crash. Nor was there a tulip shelter or its support equipment. If there were any people, surely they would have shown themselves by now. As he got closer there were deep scratches along the top of the survey vehicle. Off to the side were signs of a struggle. Jamie's breath caught in his throat, when he noticed the huge three-toed footprint stamped into the sand. Alongside, was a dark stain that spread out over the porous ground. He felt a chill run up his spine, someone had died here!

Out of the corner of his eye he caught movement through the scuffed canopy of the skimmer. For a moment he doubted what he saw. Crouching low with his spear held defensively, Jamie slowly circled the vehicle. He tried to swallow down his fear, but too many things had gone wrong since the crash. Then he saw movement again, this time he saw a head, with a distinct human eye peaking over the edge.

Lowering his spear he called out, "Hey, my name is Jamie. Who are you?"

The head ducked down out of sight again. As he watched, the head slowly peaked over the edge once more. There was definitely someone in there. Jamie called out again, "Don't be scared, I'm Jamie Chambers from Base Camp."

---

The words seemed to come from a great distance. Jamie Chambers, yes she remembered that name, but it felt like a lifetime ago, before the night of terror.

Shaking, Amanda looked carefully through the scratched canopy, squinting into the bright sunlight. A halo of gold framed the apparition's deeply shadowed features, making it hard to see his face. The tall figure came slowly towards her, making her want to hide once again. The shadowed face finally dissolved into human features with deep blue eyes that seemed to look right through her. She could see the ruggedness of his tanned face, wisps of a short dark beard, he looked more like a man than the youth she had known. She covered her face, sinking back into the seat, touching Symone's node behind her left ear for the hundredth time, but no help was forthcoming. This could not be real; nobody could be alive in this horrible land!

---

The gaunt face had disappeared behind her hands. The child must be terrified, he thought.

"Don't be afraid, I'll going to help you. I'm going to come closer to open the canopy. Is that all right?"

Terrified eyes framed in a tangled mass of greasy hair, appeared. As he stepped closer, she shook her head gesturing with her hand for him to stop. In that moment he recognized something in the thin face, could it be Amanda Martin? Holding up his hands, he said as steadily as he could, "Amanda, is that you?"

She stopped shaking her head and stared at him wide-eyed.

"You are Amanda, aren't you? Don't be afraid of me, it is quite safe out here now."

In a croaking voice, barely audible through the canopy, she said, "That's not true, terrible things have happened out there!"

Jamie looked at the skimmer's deeply scratched fuselage, seeing in better detail the evidence of the Raptor's attack. The truth of what happened here was starting to sink in, and he said in a calm voice, "Amanda you know who I am, and I assure you it is safe right now. They don't come out in the daylight, so it's all right for you to open the canopy. You know how to do that, don't you?"

Amanda moved her head up and down, and then from side to side. Confusion etched across her face, so Jamie went on, "I'm going to come up to the side of your skimmer. There is an emergency release that I can activate, but I don't want to scare you."

She just stared back at him as he slowly stepped forward, searching for the flush-mounted release. There was a barely audible thump as the back of the canopy split open. Amanda was shaking all over as he slid open the canopy. A rush of hot air wafted up past him, mingled with the smell of confinement. Amanda covered her face with her hands again.

"Come on, let me help you out of there," and on impulse he added, "Would you like a nice drink of water." She opened her hands enough to look up at him.

Jamie reached over the edge, speaking softly, "Come on now, I will not hurt you and you really need to get out of this oven." Carefully gripping her slender arm, he started to draw her out of the cockpit, but he soon realized she was too weak to assist. "Amanda, I need to get up on the skimmer to help you out of the cockpit. He took her nod as acceptance. Once he was straddling the skimmer, he reached down taking her under the armpits from behind. He was shocked at how fragile she felt. Once over the side, she struggled to stand, but her efforts were pitifully weak. Sliding down to join her, Jamie eased her under the shade of the hover wing. From his bag, he took out a full water container, offering it to her. She took a few tentative sips and then started to gulp it down.

"OK, OK, you've had enough for now. We don't want to make you sick, now do we?" he said in a gentle voice, as he took the container away.

In a small rasping voice she said, "What's the use, we'll only die anyway."

"No, we won't. I haven't died yet and you won't either!" replied Jamie.

"There are terrible things out there, I've seen them."

"You're safe right now. We'll get to an even safer place for the night." said Jamie, hoping that was true. He looked up to where Alheeza was hiding and mind-spoke: *I've found one survivor here. She is in pretty bad shape and scared witless from a Raptor attack.*

*I have been watching. Is she hurt?*

*I do not think she is hurt. Most probably she has suffered from lack of food and water.*

*Then give her some of the copeander fruit to help revive her.*

He found one of the wrinkled red fruit and cut into small pieces before handing her a section. She held it without much interest, gazing off into the distance.

"Please eat it. The fruit is like medicine." said Jamie.

She put it in her mouth, chewing slowly. Her lower lip stuck in a pouting frown, "What is this stuff?"

"It is a local fruit. I have found it revives one's strength wonderfully."

"Oh." She continued to chew. "It tastes funny."

"Where is the rest of the crew?" Jamie asked.

The thin girl started to shake again as her sunken eyes met his. "My Mom is dead! She got out of the skimmer a few nights ago to collect dew off the skimmer. That was when that thing swooped down killing her!" She started to weep. Not knowing what to do, Jamie sat down beside her, putting his arm around her. Amanda's sobs turned to wailing, as she rested her head against his chest. Instinctively, Jamie embraced her. He was not sure how long she sobbed, but finally she lay quietly against him. How strange it felt to have this girl snuggled up to him so naturally. All the time on

Mayflower he had hardly ever touched one of the females.

"I'd like to move you to a safe camp site, do you have any other clothes with you, anything you want to bring with you?"

Through sobs she managed to tell him that they'd been flying back to Base Camp. Suddenly, everything had quit and they'd been stranded with no extra supplies. Amanda reached up behind her left ear. "And my Symone quit too, I've had no way of getting my questions answered."

"I'm going to call a friend to join us. He's different from us, so please don't be afraid."

*Alheeza, please come join us*," he mind spoke.

---

*Alheeza felt apprehension as he crossed the sandy opening between the bush and the alien craft. He had grown accustomed to his new companion, but to approach another of these strange creatures made him uneasy.*

*His unease was replaced with curiosity when he saw the frail being that nestled against Jamie. Her shoulders shook intermittently while accompanied by unintelligible utterings.*

---

"Try to take another bite of the dried fruit. It really will make you feel better." said Jamie kindly.

While she chewed a small bite, he asked, "How did you survive all this time without your supplies?"

It took some time before she answered, and it was in a barely audible whisper, "W-w-we were using our emergency food and water sparingly. Mom found that she could collect the dew off the hover wing and hull of the skimmer in the early morning. She went out early one morning when it was still dark, because we were so thirsty. That is when this big black creature swooped down. I heard Mom scream, and when I looked up she was dangling from its grip as it flapped back up into the sky!"

Amanda stared off towards the stain in the sand before continuing. "I thought it couldn't get any worse after Mom died, but it came back the next night, beating on the craft. It was ......" Sobbing, Amanda buried her face in his chest again.

Jamie did not know what to do next. He sat rocking her gently back and forth until she started to sit up. Reaching over, he passed her the water bottle again, along with another slice of copeander fruit. They sat there wordlessly for a while until she noticed Alheeza seated nearby. She said, "I didn't know you had a dog!"

Jamie and Alheeza looked at each other.

*How did she come to that conclusion, and what is a dog?* mind-spoke Alheeza.

*In Earth's history, they were pets, obedient creatures that some kept as companions.*

Alheeza considered this before replying: *I do not think I like this description.*

Amanda lifted her head and looked around, "Can I pet your dog?"

Jamie and Alheeza looked at each other.

"She would like to touch you Alheeza." said Jamie.

*Must I, she does not smell very nice?*

*Come on, she really needs our help. Just let her touch you.*

*She may touch me,* mind-spoke Alheeza as he stepped closer to her.

Amanda tentatively put a hand out brushing her finger tips along the Denzel's shoulder.

"Oh my gosh, he's beautiful!" said Amanda as she stroked him along his sleek-scaled back.

"I've never touched a real dog, where did you get him?"

"He's rather special, and it's a much longer story. Right now we need to find out if you can walk, because tonight we need a safe place for all of us."

Amanda reluctantly withdrew her hand from Alheeza, as Jamie gently pulled her to her feet.

Amanda took a tentative step but had to put out a hand on the skimmer to keep from falling. Jamie quickly stepped up, holding her about the waist. She barely came to his shoulder and he could feel her ribs through the thin jump suit.

"I don't feel dizzy any more, but I still feel a bit weak," she added.

*Alheeza, you know better than me where to find a campsite that we can stay for some time. Can you scout ahead and I will follow:* mind-spoke Jamie.

*Yes, I will search back the way we came; there was a ravine that may hold promise.*

*I remember the ravine; we will follow as best we can.*

"Where is your dog going?" asked Amanda.

"Oh, he is going to look for a campsite."

"Can he really do that?"

"Yeah, he's a special dog! Shall we try a few more steps?" asked Jamie.

"All right!"

Gathering up his bag and spear, Jamie put an arm around Amanda's waist. After a few clumsy steps, Jamie found a gait that more or less matched Amanda's limited strength.

By the time they reached the hill leading back into the forest below, it was apparent that Amanda was too weak to make the ascent herself.

"When you were little, did your Mom or Dad ever give you a ride on their back?" he asked.

With a puzzled look she replied, "Oh yeah. Why?"

"We're not going to get very far unless I carry you."

"You're going to carry me?"

"Unless you have a better plan." he said shrugging.

After studying her face for a few moments, Jamie squatted down in front of Amanda and waited. Soon he felt her arms slip over his shoulders.  Carefully, he threaded his arms under her thighs. Grabbing his spear and gear bag was a little more challenging, but with his hands full and Amanda on his back, he hoisted his load. It was heavy but not impossible. If she had not lost so much weight, he couldn't have made it very far.

He searched for something to say and settled on, "How old are you?"

"Sixteen, last December, Earth time. I would turn seventeen in just a few months?"

"I just turned that in June."

"That makes us 6 months apart. Back on Mayflower you didn't hang out with the other boys much, did you?"

"No, I had other interests." replied Jamie.

Before the conversation went any farther his new charge seemed to drift off, so he trudged on looking for the ravine.

---

About half an hour later, a wobbly Jamie put Amanda down in the shade of the purple fan tree, where she continued to doze. He rubbed his burning thighs trying to work the knots out of them. He looked around the forest, admiring its multi-coloured leaves and tangled bushes. The larger trees that emerged formed a kind of tattered roof where the late afternoon sunlight streamed through in brilliant shafts. It was peaceful here.

Jamie was sipping some of the last of their water, when he heard movement behind him. Amanda had awoken, looking as if she was still in the grip of some nightmare. As their eyes met she seemed to calm a bit.

"It's OK, you just fell asleep. There is no danger here." Reaching over, he passed the water container. "Have a drink we should not have far to go now."

Nodding, she put the container to her lips, taking a long drink.

He handed her a handful of purple berries, saying, "You need more to eat if you are going to get strong."

He was rewarded with a smile as she chewed on the first mouthful. In no time Amanda had eaten all of his Acava berries. Then she tipped the water jug up and emptied it as well.

"Oh my gosh, I didn't know I was that thirsty!" gasped Amanda, as she shook the empty jug. Her eyes slowly rose to meet Jamie. "I didn't mean to drink it all. I'm sorry."

"It's OK, we'll get more soon."

She put it down, pointing, "Look, there's your dog!"

Alheeza strode through the brush, mind-speaking: *I found a place farther along the ravine that will be suitable. Can you follow me now?*

*We will try.*

Amanda insisted that she could walk, but before long it was apparent that he was going to have to carry her again.

Without any further discussion, Alheeza turned to pad off down the slope. He had not gone far, when he turned to see if Jamie was able to follow. How strange it was to see the way the aliens cared for one another. It was surprising, since he had always believed his race was the only one capable of compassion.

# The Camp

I f Jamie thought climbing up the slope was challenging that morning, it was nothing compared to his struggle to carry Amanda down the rocky hill. His legs burned from the exertion. Time passed slowly as he took one agonizing step after another, and then he heard in his head: *You are close now my friend.*

Staggering along the steep ravine, Jamie passed a large clean spring, the source of a creek that followed the ravine downhill. Not far ahead, Alheeza was waiting by some purple bushes. From their time on the trail, Jamie had started to read the subtle expressions on Alheeza's face, and thought he was smiling, having found something behind the undergrowth .

As Jamie came closer he could see why Alheeza seemed so pleased. It was a partially concealed cave with a small flat area at the entrance. How he had found it was a wonder.

As Jamie stepped through the entrance, he paused to let his eyes adjust. It was hard to tell how high the ceiling was, but it opened up into a spacious room. Carefully, Jamie let Amanda slip off his back, where she collapsed on the ground. Leaving her to rest, Jamie stepped outside to the spring, where he had a long drink of its cool water and then filled his containers.

By the time he returned, Amanda was fully awake again and thirsty. He wrapped her in his space blanket and gave her more water. Crouching with her blanket, Amanda watched Jamie's silhouette as he made several trips carrying dry branches. Taking some things from his pack, the young man struck sparks onto a small pile of branches with something fluffy. A thin spiral of smoke rose from the tinder. While Jamie blew on it, a crackling flame appeared. She was dumbfounded by how quickly he made the fire. The little blaze, near the entrance, snapped and crackled as the smoke lifted out past the opening. Curiously, he placed several small stones in a circle around the fire, and settled cross-legged beside it.

"How did you learn to do that?" she asked?

"Tom Brown's Field Guide," Jamie said pulling the old book from his bag.

"You've got a paper book? Where did you get that?"

"It was a gift handed down to me from my great-grandfather."

Amanda put her arms around her shoulders and shivered.

"Come sit by the fire, it will warm you," Jamie said in a soft voice, as he reached out a hand.

She came and settled beside him. The fire did feel good. Jamie rummaged in his bag, pulling out several white lumps. Jamie popped one in his mouth, while handing the other two over to her.

"Go ahead, eat these. They are really good," he said.

As she chewed, Amanda looked into the face of this strange young man. It was Jamie Chambers, she remembered him, but he had changed so much. Gone was the timid, skinny kid with the high voice. She looked at the rugged, tanned face with its thin dark beard. He was not a full man yet, but there was something about the sad eyes that belonged in a much older person.

Not sure where to start, she asked, "Where is your dog?"

"He is out in the forest, he'll be back soon."

"Oh!" she replied, pausing before going on, "How did you find me and where are the others?"

"What others?" Jamie replied.

"The others from the rescue team of course."

"I'm from a survey vessel, just like you. As for the others, there are none that I know of. It was just my Dad and I, just like you and your mother," said Jamie as he continued to stare into the fire.

"But where is he?" Amanda replied earnestly.

She thought he was not going to answer because all he did was look at an old silver ring on his left hand. Tears started to trickle down his checks. Finally he replied, "We crashed after the sun got really bright. My Dad and I were trying to make our way back to Base Camp, when he fell off a cliff and died in the river. That's when I met Alheeza and we have been together ever since. There are no other rescuers."

Amanda stopped chewing, a lump forming in her throat. She tried to speak, but could not form the words. All that could be heard was the snapping of the fire.

---

*Alheeza had mixed feelings about the newest member of their group. She did not exhibit the same strong telepathic signature that Jamie had, but there was still something about her. He would have to sort that out later.*

*Darkness was creeping into the forest as Alheeza searched in the undergrowth. He smelled the pungent odor of a rare delicacy. Crossing the area once more, he stopped over the strongest smelling spot. Hastily, he scratched at the base of the wiry vegetation, tearing at the fibrous soil. Through the tangle of little roots the first of the bulging tubers tumbled free. He sniffed it; 'Yes', this was it. He bit into the end of it, shutting his eyes in satisfaction as his mouth filled with the exotic flavour.*

---

It was almost totally dark when Alheeza came back to camp with several tubers dangling from his mouth.

*You have to try these?* he mind-spoke to Jamie.

"What does your dog have?" asked Amanda as Jamie took the roots from Alheeza.

"I think it's supper!" exclaimed Jamie.

"He can do that?"

"Yeah, he's special!" *Did you get that Alheeza, you are special.*

*A concession that I accept.*

Sometime later they ate slices of yellow tuber roasted on sticks by the fire. Plucking one from its cooking skewer, Jamie tossed the hot morsel from hand to hand, trying to cool it. Quickly, he snatched a bite from the end of it. Closing his eyes he said, "Oh, this is really good!"

*You spoil the taste by burning it,* mind-spoke Alheeza.

*Remember my first stewed nuts and fruit? You liked it well enough.*

*I will grant you that, but these are different. They are a delicacy favoured by our kind.*

*Well, I just thought I would try it. I think they smell even better as they roast by the fire.*

*It does not seem a proper way to treat good food.*

Jamie handed one to Amanda saying, "It's still hot, try it."

She smiled a rare smile, as she carefully took the offered food. Her eyes widened as she chewed the first mouth full. "Oh, you're not kidding, are you!" she said as she eagerly took another bite.

*Your race has some very strange habits.*

*Oh come on, try a bite yourself Alheeza.*

The young denzel sniffed the offered food. Tentatively, he licked the hot tuber. A curious expression crossed his finely scaled snout. *Interesting, it tastes sweeter this way. Our race would never have done this. Fire is something you have brought. It is another advantage of our alliance.*

*Oh I agree!* Jamie smiled back at him.

After eating their fill, Jamie looked around their little cave. Alheeza lay nearby, with his eyes half closed, and Amanda was sound asleep, wrapped in a space blanket. What a strange group they were: a lonely boy, a starved girl, and an isolated denzel, all orphaned. However, it did feel good to have eaten wholesome food, seated by a warm fire, and in the company of friends. He looked down at his father's ring, spinning the silver band with his thumb. What would his father say if he could see him now? He felt his throat tighten but this time he held back the tears. He had survived; he knew his father would be proud of that. He reached up to feel Symone's activation node behind his ear, it reminded him that he had survived without it, or any of their high tech wonders. He would go on surviving; he knew it in his bones.

---

It was well into the night, and the fire was all but out. Suddenly, Jamie awoke, vaguely aware that something had disturbed his sleep. Noticing that Alheeza was wrapped around Amanda, and both were still asleep, he quietly reached into his suit and clasped the crystal. It felt warm to his touch and somehow reassuring. He'd already noticed that when he held the stone, his senses seemed to come alive. Faint details of the cave came into focus and he could hear small creatures scurrying about in the ravine. Then, he noticed the smells: the ashes were pungent, a sweetness lingered from the roasted tubers, and the human smell of Amanda was comforting.

Then he heard it. Distant wing beats, something large was approaching. Fear shot through him, tensing his muscles and twisting his stomach.

"Wake up!" he said urgently. "We must move to the back of the cave, hurry!"

Alheeza woke instantly but Amanda did not move. Without hesitation Jamie reached under her, drawing her frail body close to him. They moved quickly to the back of the cavern.

*What is it?* mind-spoke Alheeza.

A *Raptor is approaching,* telepathed Jamie, cradling Amanda protectively.

There was a thrashing sound as the great creature landed in the brush above the ravine. Stones tumbled in front of the cave, accompanied by the scraping sounds of something large descending. Jamie's nostrils flared as the stench reached him. There was a great crashing as its bulk hit the bottom of the ravine.

Amanda stirred in his arms, "Stay still and be quiet little one." he whispered in her ear as he clutched her close.

Jamie couldn't decide whether it was the starlight or the crystal, but he could see a pair of burning red eyes glaring towards him, making him feel naked. As they stared at each other, more details became clear. The large black skull with its swept back cranial and jaw fins. Interlocking shiny scales defined a square face with a gaping jaw outlined by a double row of yellow teeth. Jamie's breath caught in his throat.

Its huge head was reaching in towards them, but soon its cranial fin caught in the low passage, blocking its progress. The cave reverberated, as it bellowed, the stench from its breath filling the space. It shook its immense head and thrust forward again, only to be stopped by the narrow passage. Three more times it tried at various angles but it was too big to cross the threshold.

One more hate-filled scream, and it drew back. As quickly as it arrived, it clambered up the hillside in a shower of stones, taking to the night sky, with thunderous strokes of its mighty wings.

When the last of the stones tumbled down, a hush fell over the ravine. Not a creature stirred, except for the stifled weeping from Amanda as she shook with intermittent spasms. All he could do was hold her tight, whispering, "It's gone, and we're safe!"

*For now!* mind-spoke Alheeza.

It was hard to tell how much time had passed, Jamie's legs and arms had fallen asleep holding his charge. She had wrapped her arms around him, burying her face in his shoulder. Some time later, fingers of amber light crept down the ravine. Morning had arrived, and they had survived yet another attack.

Jamie tried moving his right leg, but it did not respond. As he shifted sideways, pain interlaced with needles shot through his limb. It took a few moments for the circulation to return, and then he gently rolled Amanda off his lap. Wrapped in the space blanket, she continued to sleep as he stood.

Alheeza came to stand next to Jamie at the entrance, mind-speaking: *This is like the encounter under the Herman nut trees. You sensed the night killer coming then. I do not believe this is coincidental.*

Jamie continued to stare outside, but finally he responded: *I do not really know. One minute I was sound asleep, and then I was awake. I reached for the crystal, and somehow I could feel more around me. It was the sound of its distant wings that I heard first. That's when I shouted that we should move.*

Alheeza telephathed: *The real question is what was it that awakened you first? This is my world; I should have been aware of the danger before you.*

Jamie shrugged.

*Is that movement some type of communication?*

*Yeah! It means I do not know.* Jamie looked down at the crystal in his hand, sensing that the answer to the mystery was probably right in front of them.

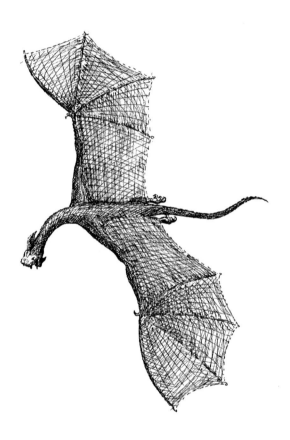

# Sanctuary

F or the next two days, Jamie and Alheeza kept themselves busy exploring the adjacent forest while Amanda continued recuperating in the cave. By now, she knew how to take care of their small fire that would keep her safe from prowling invaders.

Rocks gave way to clusters of twisted foliage as the pair of explorers ventured from their cave down the ravine that opened into the forest below. The purple and green canopy created a mottled pattern on the forest floor. As they made their way through the brush, Alheeza continued to be Jamie's guide. Nevertheless, Jamie was learning quickly about this strange land. After their encounters with the wilda-cats, he went everywhere with his spear in hand.

Well before dark the two foragers returned to their ravine with its small cave. It started to feel more homelike with its: familiar fire, smells of prepared food, and someone to greet them upon their return. They called it 'Sanctuary', for it was their first safe haven since the great technological catastrophe and the Raptor raids.

Amanda was waiting for them at the mouth of the cave. Her small fire sent up a slender column of smoke before the breeze above whisked it away. She sat cross-legged, comfortably reading his book. It was surprising to see how quickly she had come back to life. She still looked gaunt, but her eyes were clear with a sharp intelligence behind them.

"What are you reading about?" he asked.

"I've been reading about weaving with natural fibers. If I could just find something like the reeds in this book, I am sure I could make mats or even crude blankets. Wouldn't it be nice to be warm at night?" Amanda offered.

"You're right about that." he said, and then in mind-speak: *Alheeza, are there any plants near here that Amanda could strip fiber from. She wants to make something while we are out every day.*

*If you can explain what she needs more clearly, perhaps I can assist.*

The two humans continued to discuss the raw materials that would be needed for basic weaving. All the while Jamie translated the details to Alheeza.

Later that night, they rested after having eaten their fill of Herman nuts, followed by some yellow fruit that Alheeza had found. Jamie slumped by the dwindling fire, spinning the silver ring on his second finger. He did not sense Amanda stepping near him. "Do you miss him?" she asked.

Startled, he sat up, looking into her eyes. They held each other's gaze for a few moments before saying, "You mean my father?"

"Of course, I mean your father."

Jamie looked back down at the unadorned ring on his left hand. How to answer her? While he was mulling this around, Amanda broke in, "I think about my Mom all the time."

He could hear the emotion in her voice. Without thinking he started to talk, "This land, this planet, it's so strange. During the day I'm so busy that there is no time to think about losses. However, when it gets quiet, that's when I really miss him."

Jamie reached over to place another piece of dry fuel on the fire. "As I was growing up, we used to read the old book together in the evenings. He was my mentor, but something happened after the solar storm. After the crash he was really sick, and I thought he was going insane. He made some really stupid decisions, and I got angry with him, saying things I wish I hadn't. Then, just as we were starting to get along, he fell off the cliff and died." When the flames started to lick around the branch, he could see Amanda's face better. Tears dripped from her hollow cheeks, and before he knew it his hand was brushing them from her face. Her sobs came uncontrollably then. Jamie did not realize that he was weeping too. How they ended in each other's arms, neither could tell, but they clung to each other until their crying subsided.

"Where is your mother?" Amanda whispered as she eased her hold of Jamie.

"My mother, Margery, is back at Base Camp. That is if everything is all right there. And where is your father?"

"My father, oh that is a long story."

"I have the time." Jamie replied.

"Back on Earth, before our people found a way to escape, my father was a key member of the opposition movement. One night, members of the Believer's Security Force came for him. After they took him away, we never saw him again."

Jamie watched her troubled face as she recounted the story. Then in his head he added up their ages. "If he vanished before Mayflower set off, how is it that you are only 16 years of age? The mission left 19 years ago."

"I told you, my mother was a psychologist and a biologist. My parents were smart enough to know the risks my father was taking by speaking out, so they made plans."

"That still doesn't make sense to me."

"They set aside a fertilized egg, "me" in a time capsule sort of speak. After escaping Earth, my mother chose a time to carry me to term, and here I am."

Jamie just stared at her before he asked, "What were your mother and father's name?"

"Helen and Wilfred," Amanda replied, and after a moment she added, "Jamie, how are the people from Mayflower going to find us?"

"I don't like having to tell you like this, but since you asked, the Mayflower is gone too. I saw it explode upon re-entry shortly after our equipment failed. I didn't want to believe it, but on the way here we found a fragment of the hull. I'm sorry, there is no Mayflower anymore, and that means we are truly marooned here."

"Oh, Jamie!" her eyes welling with tears, "I saw it too, but I assumed it was a meteorite." Amanda started to tremble again, so Jamie took her in his arms. Finally, she whispered, "Jamie, what if we are the last people alive on this planet?"

"I've thought about that too, but the settlers should be all right. After all, they had all the start-up supplies, and surely they would have found a way to cope with the technological failures," Jamie said with more conviction than he felt.

They sat up for some time, sharing memories of their parents and life aboard the Mayflower.

*Alheeza lay as if asleep, with his one eye open a slit. In the time he had spent with the one called Jamie, he had started to understand much of their spoken language, but it was not just the words they shared, it was the feeling of grief and loss that emanated from the tall one, reflected in the skinny one, that moved him the most. These were complex creatures, not the same as his race, but communal with a need for each other, not unlike his race. He felt the pull to be reunited with his kind. It would be imperative to reach the great denzel gathering in the next moon. Even with the risk of Raptor attacks, his race would come together at the end of the warm season cycle.*

Later that night, the three survivors slept close to each other to share body heat.

# A Denzel Exposed

---

Jamie trudged up the hill toward the cave, following Alheeza. From the day's foraging, he carried a sack of tubers, nuts, fruit, and a recent favourite, acava berries. His spirits started to lift as they neared the opening in the ravine wall. Smoke curled out from the slit and Amanda sat cross-legged intently working on something. Very soon she would be ready for the long hike across country, in the hopes of finding Base Camp.

He called, "I hope you have a nice warm stew ready for a pair of weary travelers!"

Her head shot up at the sound of their approach. Standing, she waved down to them, "I thought you'd never get back. What took you so long? "

Jamie smiled at hearing her voice. The thin creature they had rescued three weeks before was unrecognizable. Washed up and several kilos heavier, she looked more like a young women than a refugee. A tingle of excitement traced through his body at seeing her.

"With that appetite of yours, we had to go farther afield to find food today."

*That is not the whole truth,* mind-spoke Alheeza.

"And I was looking for something to make a better bow." added Jamie.

*That is closer to the truth.*

"Did you find any?"

"Maybe. We'll see," he said as they reached the shelf in front of Sanctuary.

"Look what I have," she said, proudly holding up a ragged edge of woven fabric. "It's the start of our first blanket, well a mat really!"

"You're amazing! Did you do all this today?"

"Yes!" She stepped around the pile of shredded fiber, crouching to embrace Alheeza. "You are just so sweet!" she said, as she planted a kiss on the side of his smooth scaled head.

*I think you enjoy that as much as she does,* mind-spoke Jamie.

*Amanda is very acceptable now,* telepathed Alheeza as he leaned against her.

"That spoon, made into a sharpened knife, was really helpful for trimming my weaving today," she said.

"Glad it helped."

She stood, took a quick step towards him, wrapping Jamie in a light hug. "You're more than all right too." She smiled as she stepped back. "It is getting easier to stay here by myself. I have to admit, since you made me my own spear, I feel even better."

Returning her smile he said, "I am proud of you."

She embraced him firmly this time, laying her head on his chest. "I know."

In that moment he was back on the Mayflower, being hugged by his mother. She had been his only feminine touch until recently. Here everything had changed. There was still a hole inside him without his parents, and all the comforts of their technology seemed a life time ago. Now here he was, standing in the late afternoon sun, holding Amanda Martin with the smell of her hair filling his nostrils. There was a surge of excitement that pulsed through his body, and before she could feel the center of that excitement he detached himself. As he stepped back, he whispered, "You're very special to me."

Looking up into his face, she paused before saying, "Same here."

Trying to change the subject, he said, "I have something special for you." He held out his hand revealing a slender object.

"What is it?" She asked.

"With any kind of luck, it is a needle to help you finish some of your weaving."

Plucking it from his hand she held it up for inspection. "Where did you get this?"

"Alheeza showed me where I could get a broken plant that had shattered into slivers this size. It took several tries but I managed to bore a tiny hole in the end to make a passable needle." He handed over the second homemade needle, saying, "I thought two would be better than one, especially if one breaks."

She hugged him again, and then reached up to plant a kiss on his cheek.

---

Amanda had been watching Jamie and Alheeza by the fire as she threaded some thin plant fiber into her new needle, "It's almost as if you can talk to each other." she said.

*When are you going to tell her?* mind-spoke Alheeza. They had been skirting around this topic for weeks now.

*I don't really know how to explain it. She has never really picked up any of our feelings or thoughts in the same way you did.*

*True, but she does need an explanation. I am sure the "dog" theory of my existence is growing thin.*

*True.*

"See what I mean, it is like you have some kind of silent communication with him." Amanda interjected.

"Well that is closer to the truth than you may have guessed." started Jamie.

"Aha! I knew it!"

"You see, if it wasn't for Alheeza, I would never have survived on this planet at all. He watched Dad and me after we crashed. I got feelings from him. Feelings about where to find water and food, and after Dad died, I found this." Jamie pulled the gleaming red crystal from his suit.

Amanda eyes shone with excitement as she said, "I've seen you wearing it, and it's gorgeous. Can I touch it?"

Jamie looked down at his precious stone before saying, "It has certain properties that I did not understand at first. Here let me show you something else." From his waist pack he drew out the amber crystal.

Amanda looked startled. "Do you hear some kind of music?"

"When I found the red one, I heard music."

Amanda stared at the pair of crystal gems. Tentatively she reached forward, placing a finger upon his stone. A look of curiosity etched her face, but Jamie felt none of the telepathic connection he had hoped for.

Amanda reached for the amber stone. At the moment her finger made contact, she jumped in shock.

What was going on here, she thought to herself?

Tentatively she touched the amber stone again. This time there was no bolt of energy, just a warm tingling as her finger grasped the stone. The moment she made full contact the music stopped. When she looked up, Jamie's eyes were iridescent and he seemed to shimmer. It was not just his physical appearance, he seemed to radiate feelings. It was like she became fluent in his body language that made his every emotion visible. There was a jumble of grief and guilt around his father, a longing to find his mother, frustration at some of the things he was trying to make, but there was a hidden love for her along with a burning passion. More layers were becoming visible, but taking a deep breath, Amanda dropped the stone. Suddenly, everything in the cave returned to normal and Jamie was just a young man in a worn jumpsuit.

She picked the stone up again, glancing about. When her gaze settled upon Alheeza, her mouth dropped open, as he shimmered before her. Then came an array of feelings: intelligence, mourning his lost ones, a deep bond with Jamie and with her also.

*Can you see me now?* came a thought in her head.

"I can see you in every way!" she said as she crouched in front of Alheeza. "Oh, can I see you! You're beautiful!"

*Now how can I argue with an intelligent being like this?* mind-spoke Alheeza.

It was like Amanda was hit with an electric shock, the way she jumped. "Oh, shit!" she exclaimed uncharacteristically.

*I think the denzel is out of the bag, so to speak,* Jamie added.

"Crap! Who is doing this?" exclaimed Amanda.

*We are both sending our thought messages to you, Amanda Martin.*

Amanda looked visibly shaken. "You two really do talk. I mean, he isn't what I thought he was at all!" She turned to Jamie, "And you let me refer to him as your dog, for what, weeks?"

Blushing, Jamie hung his head before mind-speaking: *It seemed easier at the time, after all the concept of an Earth-like dog was in all of the history holograms. You were in really rough shape and you liked him as a dog, didn't you?*

*I was never flattered about being called a dog,* protested Alheeza.

As fast as her temper flared, it was gone. She held the crystal and looked at Alheeza. *What are you really?* she asked, not realizing that she had slipped into mind-speak.

*I am a denzel. We are an ancient race that has dwelt here since the beginning of time. As Jamie said, we became partners in survival after my genetic elders and his father were killed. With the knowledge passed down to me about the life on this planet together with Jamie's ability to use tools, we have fared very well together. Now you are here too, and that is how it is.*

*How is it that I can hear you now in my head?* she asked.

*I think it is the power of the crystal,* mind-spoke Jamie.

"Does it work with all crystals?"

*After watching you with my ruby stone, and then how you responded to the amber one, I would have to say no. For some reason I am in tune with the red one, but you seem connected to the amber one. This is exceptionally good luck!*

*Why did you not show me these marvellous crystals before?* continued Amanda.

Jamie exchanged glances with Alheeza. *We have been trying to find a way to break it to you. I was afraid we would scare you, especially if the crystals did not work for you. This whole telepathic communication does not fit the scientific model. I did not want you to go screaming from the cave.*

*Oh ye of little faith!* she exclaimed as she reached up on tip toes to place a full kiss upon Jamie's lips.

Turning, she left the dazed Jamie standing bewildered and kneeled to hug Alheeza. *I still think you are the greatest, my little friend.*

# The Naked Truth

———————◯———————

Two days later, Jamie had forgotten his water container back at Sanctuary, and was making his way along the stream when he heard Amanda singing somewhere ahead. Her voice was like magic, the way it rose and fell in smooth melodic tones. As her voice grew stronger, it was interlaced with splashing. The first thing he saw was the sum total of her wardrobe hanging from slim branches, apparently freshly washed. On occasion she had to wear one of his oversized jump-suits while cleaning her own. This must be one of those days.

A glimpse of her through the fan bushes left him frozen in place. She was standing naked in the stream with her back to him. His first impulse was to turn away as quickly as he could, but he couldn't take his eyes off her. There was no doubt she had been transformed from the skeletal creature a few weeks ago into something new. Still very slender by Mayflower standards, the intersecting curves were that of a young woman. An involuntary smile traced across his lips, as well as tingling further down.

Conjuring up all his courage, he turned to leave, but stumbled on a loose stone in his haste. Grabbing a slender branch to catch himself, he accidentally kicked a few stones free where they clattered over the edge of the stream bed.

"Jamie? I sure hope that is you!" she exclaimed.

"Yep, it's me all right!"

"Good, I'm glad I don't have to face a gang of wilda-cats on my own today."

With his back turned to her, he could hear her splashing ashore and rummaging among her things.

"I thought you were out foraging with Alheeza?" she asked as she pulled on the oversized jump-suit, rolling up the long sleeves as she walked.

"How did you know it was me?" Jamie asked, as he slowly turned towards her again.

"It was a process of elimination really. Who else lives around here? OK, maybe it's Jamie!" she smiled as she advanced to where he stood.

Jamie trembled; this was completely new ground for him. Even Alheeza had telepathed: *I sense something changing within you. Our race takes one mate in a lifetime; I sense this is your time?*

"OK, you caught me, I didn't mean to glimpse you bathing," he answered.

"Look, it was bound to happen sooner or later. After all, there aren't that many of us around."

"I just..." Jamie stammered as he stared at his feet. "I wasn't trying to spy on you."

"Look at me," she said.

Slowly he raised his chin, meeting those intense green eyes.

"You may be older than I am by six months, and you have been my protector since my rescue, but there are things I understand better than you. After all, girls mature earlier than boys. Now let me lay the facts out as I see them: you are a boy and I am a girl, do you follow me so far?"

Jamie nodded.

"Also, we are marooned here, maybe the last people alive for all we know, living in very close proximity to each other every day. Now given that, if you didn't find me attractive, I'd say I had a bigger problem." She grinned up at him.

*You definitely do not have a problem!* mind-spoke Jamie.

*Nor do you!* And she flashed him the biggest smile.

"How do you know all about this?"

"You studied mostly science and how to make things. My world was about people, and what they were like. After all, my Mom was a psychologist as well as a biologist. She always talked about the human journey and maturation."

"Yeah, you're probably right about that. But still how did you know I was attracted to you?" he asked sincerely.

"First, you talk in your sleep, and when I first held my crystal I could sense not only your grief but also how you feel about me. It was like the stone gave me insight into your feelings, not thoughts, just impressions.

"It did?"

"Yes, but I have to admit I think you are a bit of a hunk too."

"Oh!" Jamie was stunned and couldn't think of anything to say.

"Just come over here and let me kiss you, and it's fine if you kiss me back."

Jamie felt a tingle of excitement spread through his body.

"Well?" she said.

Steeling himself, he stepped forward, but before he could prepare himself, she took his face in her hands bringing his lips down to hers. The contact was so soft and moist and wonderful. An avalanche of excitement coursed through him. He tried to regain control of himself. Was it his shaky hands or did he feel her quiver just before pushing back.

Looking from side to side, Amanda said, "OK, we had better take this slowly, right?"

Not knowing where the words came from Jamie stammered, "I love you."

"Oh, I know you love me, you big dumb guy. I think I've loved you ever since you rescued me."

Feeling thrilled, all he could do was nod.

# The Uninvited Guest

Amanda was sitting cross-legged by her small fire, deftly working some purple leaf strands into the woven panel in her lap. She had been thinking of the previous night with Jamie holding her close as they slept. His warmth was their only real blanket, and once the fire died it became quite chilly. But it was not his warmth she was thinking about today, it was how her heart would race every time she saw him return. He set her tingling, with his lopsided grin and piercing blue eyes.

Absentmindedly, she reached to feel the amber crystal that nestled between her breasts on its thin cord. This was her link to the two most important members of the group. For Jamie she could sense his deeper feeling, and with Alheeza it was a direct way to communicate. How strange it was to find all of this normal.

A noise in the ravine startled her from her reverie. Looking up she could see Jamie's head approaching above the low brush of the narrow gully. "Hey! What did you bring me today, big guy?"

His lop sided grin brought back those feelings again. Standing, she tried to shake off the yearning while she brushed the loose fibers from her jump-suit. Instead of stopping Jamie strode past into the cave. "Hey, is that all I get for a hello today?" she called after him.

"I'll be right back! I just wanted to drop some of these things I've gathered first."

He emerged a few moments later, still looking very pleased with himself. Plopping himself beside her, he handed over a thin red strand, mind-speaking.

"Take a look at this stuff, Amanda. Alheeza showed me a tree that drips sap from broken branches. As the sap cures, it becomes incredibly stretchy. He calls it a "marvoso." Give this piece a try."

Experimentally she stretched the little filament, only to have one end slip. It snapped back, cracking her on the knuckles. "Ouch!"

Having got exactly the reaction he wanted, Jamie grinned. "Yes, isn't it the greatest stuff? I climbed that stupid tree, trying to reach some of the larger drippings and just as I got a good grip on a big one, I slipped. It's a good thing this stuff is tough, because I got the wildest ride back down to the ground before the sap broke." Holding up his left hand, Amanda could see a large red welt on his knuckles.

"You got smacked too?"

"Yes!" he replied, nodding his head with a sheepish grin that also expressed triumph.

"Have you got some idea up your sleeve about how we could use it?"

"You bet I do!" he replied. "You know how I've been trying to make a bow and arrow. The problem is I haven't found any wood that keeps its strength after it is bent for a few days. I think this elastic sap could make a very good force for driving a projectile."

"My clever fellow! You're always trying to make something from nothing."

"That's me!" he replied with pride.

She reached over and placed a hand on his arm. As their eyes met, she felt a vibration of excitement rise between them. The kiss that followed was not tentative at all. It lingered as they moved closer.

---

That night in the darkening cave, while the coals of their fire grew dim, Jamie lay awake upon their mattress of loose reeds, unable to sleep. Amanda was clutched in his arms as usual, her coarse hand-woven blanket of shredded reeds flung over them like a limp rug. She was hugging Alheeza to her chest as they all sought each other's warmth. Despite his growing attraction to Amanda, he was usually so tired by the time they lay together that sleep would eventually follow, but not tonight. At first, he thought it was just his growing passion for this slender young woman, but then a twinge of fear crept up his spine like ice water. With his free hand, he reached for his crystal slung around his neck. What he was searching for, he did not know. With dread, he sensed the wing beats of an approaching Raptor. Carefully, he reached out with his mind, seeking Alheeza: *A Great Raptor approaches.*

Instantly, his companion was alert. *How far away?*

*It sounds as if the great creature is circling somewhere high overhead.*

Jamie could feel Amanda stirring out of sleep. Surely the Raptor would leave them alone having found the cave too small the last time. That is, if it was the same Raptor. Time passed slowly as the night hunter continued to fly in orbits far above. Then all was quiet. Jamie hoped that it might have left their area, but suddenly he heard the rapid wing beats of deceleration, followed by the shower of falling stones, dislodged from the ridge above.

Amanda burst awake, sitting up in the darkness. "No, no, no! Keep that thing away from me!" she screamed. Jamie put his arms around her, whispering, "Quiet my little one, don't draw any more attention to us! Now help me move to the back of our cave."

More stones fell, as a heavy body climbed down the steep slope. When it reached the bottom, a huge dark head with piercing red eyes looked within the cave. It did not try to enter; it just stared into their cave, breathing heavily through its brow nostrils.

Amanda started to whimper, so Jamie pulled her closer, mind-speaking: *Not a sound little one.*

Somehow, she stopped whimpering.

It thrust its head forward as if to drive it into the cave, only to scream its rage at the threshold. The cave shook, as it filled with the stench of its foul breath. Then the night killer withdrew, clawing its way up the steep ravine wall. Soon all that could be heard was its departing wingbeats. All was quiet outside.

"Will this never end? Amanda whispered.

"I don't know, but we're still safe in here." Jamie answered.

*But what about when we leave this place? t*elepathed Amanda.

*I am working on that!*

*From my ancestral memories, I can tell you that it does end. I just do not know how long the killing will go on before they leave us in peace:* mind-spoke Alheeza.

*Are you saying that they come in cycles?* mind-spoke Amanda.

*Absolutely.*

Amanda rolled over to face Jamie, their bodies pressed closely together. Any other time this would have been thrilling for Jamie but now with the recent attack, it only felt comforting to have close contact.

"How will we be safe, traveling across country to find Base Camp?" she whispered.

*Alheeza, assures me that his race have found places, with reasonable cover, throughout the land.*

*It is true, we do have a network of safe places, but I cannot give you complete assurance of safety with the vigorous nature of these last killing cycles.*

*I wish that was more reassuring,* added Amanda.

"Amanda, Alheeza has kept me safe for over a month."

*And with Jamie's fire, there is more security than before I joined with him.*

All was quiet for the rest of the night. Sleep did not come easily. She shook from time to time recalling the past encounters. Each time Jamie held her firmly, sometimes stroking her hair. When she finally fell asleep, he tenderly kissed the top of her head. It was nearly dawn before he fell asleep.

# When the Forest Shakes

---

They were standing on an unfamiliar trail about an hour from Sanctuary. Far above them, the sunlight stabbed through the purple and green canopy creating shafts of light that filled the gap between the high branches and the scruffy bushes below. Amanda shuffled her feet, looking from side to side into the forest. Little could be seen through the foliage ahead.

"How do you find your way through this?" she asked.

"It's mostly Alheeza that finds our way. He has an uncanny sense of direction."

Jamie looked Amanda up and down. She stood with her shoulders back, a collection bag over one shoulder, and her short spear held butt down as a walking stick. Her lean, strong female body was well defined by the thin jump-suit. Jamie's own body started to react and he quickly turned away.

*Take the narrow trail to the left; it will lead us back in a wide circle to Sanctuary,* mind-spoke Alheeza.

"All right, I can do this!" she said through clenched teeth.

Before Jamie could say another word, she strode off along a faint trail that led deeper into the woods. Alheeza and Jamie fell in behind her.

At almost a jog, she reached the fork in the trail where she hesitated. The undergrowth was so thick here that it was difficult to see the trail ahead.

*Just follow me:* mind-spoke Alheeza as he padded off in front of her.

*What a day it has been,* thought Amanda. *Alheeza had introduced the use of so many new plants to her. She had also seen such a diversity of wild life, both big and small.*

Her muscles ached from the trek, but it felt good to travel with these two. Her honour guard, as she thought of them, kept a close formation as they threaded along the trails of this strange planet. Like Jamie, she had come to think of Alheeza as one of them. The oddity of their relationship had been replaced with a familiar comfort.

The forest had been mostly level and they were making their way down one of the gentle slopes when Alheeza stopped. He looked around, his large eyes scanning the sparsely-treed grade.

*Quickly, follow me to the cluster tree to our right.*

Amanda, hesitated looking around, but Jamie grabbed her arm saying, "Now!"

Jolted from her spot, Amanda ran with Jamie. Alheeza was already clambering into the thickly-tangled trunks of the cluster tree. Jamie pushed Amanda up after him. The overlapping interior branches made climbing easy. Alheeza stopped a few meters up, gazing down the gentle slope.

*What do you hear?* mind-spoke Amanda.

*I feel them, more than hear them,* Alheeza responded.

Sure enough, she could feel a trembling within the trunk of the cluster tree that coincided with a low rumble. Soon crashing could be heard, like trees being knocked over.

*What is coming?* she inquired.

*Swamp bellowers, a large herd by the feel of it,* Alheeza mind-spoke.

A tingling sense of dread crept up her spine; without realizing it, her hand reached out for Jamie.

Branches snapped as heavy feet pounded through dry leaves. Suddenly, the forest in front of them shook as dozens of the huge beasts burst through the foliage. Their giant bodies hammered past the hiding place. The cluster tree shook, while dust rose as the enormous beasts pressed past. Amanda blinked in disbelief as the armored herd thundered on up the slope, their pale orange bodies vanishing through the swaying trees. Leaves fluttered down through the settling dust while the forest grew quiet again.

Jamie let go of his grip on her. Amanda had not realized that she had been completely enfolded in his arms until that moment. Pressing the amber stone to her chest, she mind-spoke, *Is it like this every time you go out?*

*No, not at all! We rarely even see them at a distance.*

Without hesitation she continued: *Did you see their great horny heads? They must have a dozen or more horns sticking out all around.*

Alheeza mind-spoke: *They have exactly 13 horns. It never varies. Shall we continue now?*

As they followed him down the hill, Amanda said, "They leave an easy trail to follow."

"And they scare away everything in their path. We should have a quiet time of it for a while," added Jamie.

---

In the early afternoon, Amanda staggered under her bag of tubers, nuts, and fruit. She mind-spoke: *I do not know if I can climb the hill to Sanctuary.*

*Give me your bag,* responded Jamie.

Suddenly, Alheeza stopped in front of them. The scales on either side of his shoulder spines started to bristle.

*Wilda-cats, several of them!*

Amanda looked around, her senses suddenly on high alert. Was there something foul in the air? Jamie leaned close, whispering. "Stand to the left side of Alheeza and hold your spear at waist level."

All of her fatigue seemed to vanish as she dropped into a crouch, scanning the foliage for any signs of the attackers. She heard Jamie slide his pack to the ground, but focused on the forest. Just then three stocky, dark creatures stepped out of the brush. The larger one stood about the same height as a denzel, but much heavier through the chest. Their heads hung low, with plated lips folded up, revealing long yellow teeth. The bristling scales along the back made them look even bigger. Slowly, they advanced towards the trio snarling in guttural tones.

*It is a female with her hunting offspring, the most dangerous kind.*

The hunted and the hunters stared each other down for what felt like an eternity. Out of the corner of her eye, Amanda saw Jamie stand to his full height, drawing his arm back with his heavy spear. What happened next was a blur of movement as the larger cat charged forward. Jamie heaved his weapon. It happened almost too fast to see, but the shaft caught the attacker high on its shoulder. It spun around, apparently confused at the weapon sticking out of its side.

*Give me your spear!* Jamie mind-spoke as he snatched away Amanda's weapon. The two other wilda-cats stayed back as Jamie strode forward, driving the second spear deeply into the predator's neck. Its scream ended in a gurgling sound while it twitched on the trail, black blood oozing from its wounds.

Jamie stepped over it, drawing his crystal. Raising both arms he shouted at the two remaining wilda-cats. "**Get out of here now, you miserable creatures! Get!**"

With that and maybe the smell of their dying mother, the two offspring turned to flee into the undergrowth.

*Did you know the young ones would retreat?* mind-spoke Alheeza.

*Let us say that I hoped they would,* telepathed Jamie.

Amanda shuddered.

After retrieving their spears, Jamie came back putting an arm around her.

*How did you hit that moving creature like that?* Amanda mind-spoke.

*I would like to say that it was my superior skills, but in truth I think it was luck.*

As they passed the still body of the predator, Amanda winced.

Alheeza sniffed the limp wilda-cat, and looked up at Jamie. *I think you are now the hunter, not the hunted.*

Amanda stood clutching her spear, looking up and down the trail.

*Amanda is ready for the trek overland! Now I am hungry,* mind-spoke Alheeza as he padded off in the direction of Sanctuary.

It was very quiet that night at Sanctuary. Everyone seemed to keep their thoughts to themselves. The two humans were arranging and sorting the collected items that could best be used on their overland trek.

After a while, Jamie picked up one of his green iron-wood branches and started to whittle. "This knife's getting dull again," he muttered to himself. He picked up his best sharpening stone and started to work the edge of his knife. "I'm going to wear it out at the rate we use it."

Amanda looked up mind-speaking: *What will you do when it is worn too much to use any more?*

*In the book it shows how to sharpen certain kinds of rock. Alheeza, I hope you can help find some rocks that might work.*

*You must explain it better to me and only then will I be able to tell.*

Jamie pulled out his family's old book, thumbed his way to the familiar pages and started to read in mind-speak.

After he had finished, Alheeza telepathed: O*n the way to the great denzel gathering, perhaps there is something that will serve.*

Amanda and Jamie both stopped what they were doing.

*What great denzel gathering?* telepathed Amanda.

*I have mentioned the gathering before. I must rejoin my race, there is much that must be shared. After that, we can proceed to your Base Camp.*

Jamie mind-spoke: *I thought only you were going to your race's gathering; you make it sound like we are accompanying you.*

*We have found things that are mutually beneficial to our races, have we not?*

*Yes, I would say that,* telepathed Jamie.

*It is not far out of our way and then afterwards we can proceed to your Base Camp. It will be the most expedient way for me to explain my involvement with your kind. You two will be the ambassadors for your race. After all, I will vouch for you, if asked.*

The humans looked at each other. Shrugging Jamie mind-spoke: *Yes, our collaboration has been useful.*

*I do not know how I feel about all of this!* protested Amanda telepathically.

The other two turned to look at her.

*Well, did anyone ask if I wanted to go?*

Alheeza rose and took a step towards her: *It would please me if you, Amanda, would travel with me to the place of my ancestors gathering.*

Not answering right away, Amanda looked at her two friends. They could not have been more dissimilar. *All right, I agree,* grinning at them both.

# Leaving Sanctuary

It had been over a month since they came to this cave. Sanctuary had been a place of healing for her. In the weeks she had been here, the sounds of her mother's screaming no longer dominated her waking hours. Jamie and Alheeza had brought back hope into her life. Alheeza was the most surprising creature ever; he sat at the edge of their camp gazing up towards the crest of the hill. Soon they would start the arduous climb that would take them past her skimmer and beyond to people at Base Camp. Shaking her head, she tried to dispel any doubts about their survival.

A small fire crackled at the cave entrance warding off the morning chill. Soon the sun would climb high above the ravine, burning off the dew. With the lack of rain, the plants had taken on a permanently wilted look over the weeks. Alheeza had assured Amanda that the summer was short but intense. The fall rains would renew the forest, as they always had.

*Alheeza had been standing watch, even before the lighting of the morning fire. Now, the flames warmed his back as he scanned the ravine above them. He reflected upon the changes in the past moon cycles, and how he had encountered the strange beings. Now he shared their fire, fought with them, ate with them, and shared body heat in the cold of the night. Would his race understand this strange relationship? How he had become bonded with the aliens would alarm the elders, but in his heart, he knew it was this bond that had kept him alive.*

*Nevertheless, he felt insecure about taking the lead for he had not finished his full memory training. He had been along part of this route, but there were sections that were more conjecture than real memories. And he found it difficult to share his insecurities with Jamie, and especially Amanda.*

*Alheeza, will these containers of water be enough for us to cross the plateau above?* mind-spoke Jamie as he set aside the rigid survival containers as well two soft clear bags of water.

*That is my best estimate.*

*That is good enough for me.* And then silently, Alheeza thought to himself, "*I hope it is enough.*"

Amanda busied herself clearing away the leftovers from their breakfast. Looking up, she saw Jamie in his rough vest of coarsely woven fan bush. She had not noticed until now how the new garments seemed to make him blend in with the shrubs around them. Her time weaving had yielded many useful things, their sleeping blanket being the most useful. The cold nights had been easier to bear since she had finished it. True, it did not cover more than their torsos but the added warmth had been wonderful. Using coarse ropes made from the same fiber she had fashioned simple carrying packs that housed their drinking cans, collection bags and other small items of use.

Her gaze fell upon Jamie again: his long dark brown hair brushing his shoulder, the wisp of a beard tracing his jaw, dark skin from days in the open, and muscles that rippled up his arm as he bent to his task. It made her heart beat faster just watching him. Ever since the day by the stream, she felt drawn to him in a way that was growing ever more exciting. His touch lit a fire within.

"Have you got your pack ready?" Jamie asked.

"I've had it packed since yesterday afternoon."

She looked down at his bare feet with their thick calluses. Her shoes had not broken down yet, and she hoped they would withstand the vigorous hike up to the plateau. Jamie hoisted his considerably larger woven pack, that included their sleeping roll, shifting the weight until he was happy with his burden. Then he picked up his well-worn spear, flinger and its cluster of attached arrows. Amanda smiled at the young man in front of her. In the past two months, their lives had changed so much. They were no longer dependent upon their neuro-electronics. Before the solar storm, their technology had answered their every question, as well as providing a comfortable living environment. Now Jamie stood before her like some stone age man, resurrected from the past.

"OK, let's be off then!" Jamie said.

Settling her pack, she reached for her smaller, but no less sharp spear. She thought, if Jamie was her stone age man, then she was his stone age woman? And then she paused, looking at Alheeza, and realized what a remarkable companion he was.

Seeing the look on her face, Jamie asked, "What are you thinking?"

"Oh, I was just picturing how we have changed. Don't we look a sight, you and me in these rough vests, carrying spears like ancient people? I was just seeing us and how we have changed, that's all."

"Yeah. We must look a sight, but it feels right, doesn't it?"

"Oh, yes!"

*Let us start the ascent,* mind-spoke Alheeza. *There is plenty of time to visit on the way.*

*You are right,* telepathed Amanda.

Soon they were climbing the steep rugged slope that led back up to the dry valley above. She shuddered at the thought of passing even at a distance, the place where she had witnessed the killing of her mother. Just the thoughts of that place dragged at her feet, making her burden heavier.

As they climbed, the trees started to thin out revealing large patches of blue sky. On any other day, this would have lifted her spirits. Small spiny creatures darted about the larger rocks, chirping their territorial challenge from the safety of the cracks. Soon they were clambering through boulders that took all of her attention to keep from slipping. As she heaved herself over the rocky shelf, the whole valley opened up in front of her.

"Where is it?" she asked.

Knowing exactly what she meant, Jamie pointed off to the west. He and Alheeza had planned a route that would swing well away from the crippled skimmer.

"Isn't there anything we could use from the skimmer?" she continued.

"Alheeza and I came back here a few weeks ago. I took a few bits and pieces but there was nothing of any size we could use."

*And you did not think it was important to tell me about that?* She broke into mind-speak, as her face flushed red.

*Amanda, you were still very weak. Jamie was only trying to protect you from further pain.*

Amanda folded her arms, shifting her gaze from one to the other. Even in her rage, she could see they were only trying to spare her agony. As her breathing settled, she mind-spoke, *I am sorry, things happened here that I wish I could forget.*

Alheeza and Jamie looked at each other. With a shrug, Jamie continued, "We have all we need for the journey: lots of food, warmer clothing, and bedding, as well as better protection. What more could we need from your damaged skimmer? All that technology is dead."

Amanda reached up behind her ear, feeling the slight rise of her implant. "Yeah, you're right about that. OK, let's keep on."

---

The valley was almost devoid of vegetation. After the thick forest, this was a desert in every way. Alheeza had told her the night before that they needed to cross the dry valley in less than two days. He pointed out that the lack of drinking water along their route was the prime problem.

Amanda looked across the valley with its waves of sand dunes interspersed with rocky ridges that stood out like rows of worn teeth. In the distance, she could see a black line across the horizon, with a jagged line of gray mountains standing beyond that. It had all seemed so easy to walk to Base Camp, but looking at what lay ahead made her feel tired and their journey had just begun.

As if reading her mind, Alheeza mind-spoke, *It looks like a great distance, but we should be able to make it across in two days.*

*I hope so!* telepathed Amanda.

Jamie stood there, squinting into the distance. It really did look like a formidable challenge. Then he shrugged before saying, "Who said every long journey starts with the first step?"

---

The sun had passed its peak, bringing the hope of a cooler evening. Jamie pulled his drinking vessel from the pack. Shaking it, he estimated they had used almost half their water and they still had tomorrow to get through.

The rest of the afternoon was a long series of coarse sandy hills that sapped the traveler's strength, as they slogged along them.

As the sun dipped towards the western horizon, Jamie was feeling the full weight of his oversized pack puffing up another sandy dune. Looking over at Amanda, he saw the same utter exhaustion on her face.

*Where can we camp tonight Alheeza?* he mind-spoke.

*The memories handed down from my ancestors lead me to a place not far from here.*

Amanda shrugged, looking over at Jamie with doubt scribbled all over face.

"If Alheeza thinks it's the best we have, then it's the best."

Silently they trudged on through the shifting sand. As the sun neared the horizon another rocky ridge rose before them. It looked much like others before it, except that this one had different colored layers of sedimentary rock. At the bottom was an undercut space, like the start of a cave.

*What cut the stone like that Alheeza?* Jamie asked.

*The sand storms.*

*Sand storms?* telepathed Amanda.

*They also make the dunes we walk upon.*

*What exactly is a sand storm?* Jamie mind-spoke.

*Extremely high winds that whip the sand into the air, stripping away rock. It can be hard to breathe; survival is sometimes questionable.*

Amanda looked startled, she asked: *We have walked all day across these dunes, and now you tell us we are at risk of dying in a sand storm?*

*There was no risk today. It is tonight we have to worry. See the clouds in the east?*

Jamie and Amanda turned as one to gaze into the distance. There was a low grey cloud clinging to the horizon.

*We should make haste,* mind-spoke Alheeza as he padded towards the shelf.

Apparently, Amanda had renewed energy from the way she was trotting after Alheeza. Fatigue forgotten, Jamie picked up his pace to follow the others.

It didn't take long for them to close the distance to the sheltered overhang. The sand dune dropped sharply in front of it blocking the view to the horizon. Quickly they put their gear in the back of the overhanging rock.

*Do we make a fire with the little bit of fuel I brought?* Jamie mind-spoke.

*I was wondering about that too,* added Amanda.

*I do not understand the properties of your fire like you do. All I can say is that as darkness falls we are still at risk from above. The storm will be here in 1000 of my breaths. Your way of telling time is still foreign to me.*

*I think that is about an hour, more or less,* mind-spoke Jamie.

While the darkness crept up from the eastern horizon, the sky was gradually filled with an array of stars. Preserving his fuel, Jamie made a very small fire. Upon the desert plateau, the heat quickly dissipated leaving a chill to the air. After a cold meal of nuts and dried fruit, Amanda crawled to the back. She said sleepily, "Come on you two I need you to keep me warm."

Pulling the coarse blanket about them, Jamie and Alheeza lay awake watching the star lit sky.

It was almost as if they had expected it, for the roar of a distant Raptor came echoing over the dunes.

Jamie clutched his crystal close to his chest to bring it in contact with his skin. He had become accustomed to the enhanced senses that came with it. Still, it was sobering to see the shape of the approaching predator. He reached out to drop two twigs onto the hot coals. Blowing steadily, he was rewarded with a small flame. Adding one of his last dry branches, he continued to blow. Small as it was, the growing flame lit their rocky backdrop and the dunes in front of them.

The night hunter screamed again, banking into a tight turn. Jamie released his breath, surprised that he had been holding it. He felt Amanda's arms reach around him. Then he heard the approaching wind. Scanning the sky he sensed, rather than saw the departing Great Raptor. Was it his small fire or the approaching storm that drove it off?

Alheeza mind-spoke: *The storm is almost here!*

Jamie quickly scooped sand onto the flames. They were plunged into darkness as the first blast of abrasive wind slammed into the rock face. Amanda pulled him close and he felt the blanket pulled over him. The three of them clung together with the coarsely woven fabric their only protection against the storm.

# The Valley of Desolation

Amanda gasped awake. It was like she was being smothered. The sleeping rug pressed heavily upon her in the darkness. Jamie's usual embrace now felt like a wrestlers grip. Panic welled up in her as she squirmed to get free. At the same time, Jamie stirred behind her, groaning. As he levered himself upright, sand streamed off the rough sleeping blanket. Shafts of sunlight pierced through their confinement.

Taking long deep breaths of the morning air, helped to clear her head. She climbed to the top of the reshaped dune in front of them. A cornice of fragile sand, crumbled under her feet as she stood on the ridge. The sun cast long golden shadows between the dunes. Before her, long swells of sand spread out like some seascape frozen in time. The terror of the screaming sandstorm had passed, leaving behind a scene so quiet that it made her wonder if the whole thing had been just another nightmare.

"Are you all right?" whispered Jamie from behind her.

"I thought I was suffocating!" she replied.

"Let's get our gear so we can cross this desolation."

*And have something to eat first,* mind-spoke Alheeza.

*Yes, we need our strength for another long day, do we not?* mind-spoke Amanda.

While they walked back to camp, she said. "Oh crap, I feel like I have sand in places sand was never meant to be!"

"Me, too!" added Jamie.

They had not traveled far before they found themselves at the edge of a glistening black expanse, that undulated into the distance.

*Why do these hills look polished, Alheeza? mind-spoke Jamie.*

*I do not know how to describe it in your terms, but the ground is hard. So hard that the sun reflects off it like it was a pool of water. My race calls this the Valley of Desolation.*

Jamie looked down at his callused feet, wondering if they were up to the task ahead. *What an apt name. Is this going to be hard on our feet?*

*That is affirmative.*

*That is reassuring,* mind-spoke Amanda.

*Watch where I step, and follow carefully,* telepathed Alheeza.

It was as if a giant had combed the surface, leaving parallel wavy grooves. Sand still clung to the recesses. Devoid of plants or loose stones, it was just a stark landscape that stretched beyond the horizon. Heat waves already distorted the mountains beyond.

After a while, Jamie stopped, unslinging his pack so he could remove his coarse vest. Sweat dripped from the end of his nose as he bent to pick up his gear. Squinting into the sun, it felt as if this black expanse was a roasting skillet, here to test their true endurance. While he stood there, his callused feet started to sting from the hot surface. Striding off, he reached for and shook his water bottle.

"Shit, we are almost out of water," he muttered.

He quickened his pace to catch up to the other two.

Ahead, Amanda lurched, mumbling something before she bent to examine her left foot. "Shit!" he heard more clearly, as he came up beside her. When she moved her foot, it left a small red spot on the ground. "That doesn't look good," she muttered.

"Just sit, so I can remove your shoe," Jamie said.

Amanda's foot stung as he slid the thin unit off her foot. "What are we going to do?" she asked with a quiver in her voice.

Jamie slid his bulky load off his back, enabling him to search a side pouch. He came up with a withered copeander fruit. Using his knife, he sliced off a portion of the healing plant. First, he chewed a small piece before placing it onto the cut. Then after some more rummaging, he came up with a folded leaf with red sticky stuff pressed inside it. Carefully, he peeled some of the gooey concoction away from the leaf, smearing it over the cut. Then he put a section of the leaf over that. The shoe was replaced and drawn closed.

"OK, try stepping on that."

To her surprise, it didn't hurt as much. *How did you know how to do that?*

*Alheeza taught me about this plant, and the rest I just kind of made up.*

*You're marvelous!* she mind-spoke. Reaching up she planted a firm kiss upon his chapped lips.

---

*Aheeza always found it comforting to watch the caring behavior of the aliens. They were so much different from what the elders feared.*

*Then his thoughts shifted to the problems at hand. All morning the heat had been increasing, and with it an unaccustomed doubt crept into his mind. There were limits to his own endurance, and he had no experience with his alien friend's limitations. This area had changed at about the time of the last Great Raptor cycle, and that meant that he had no ancestral memories to aid him. All he knew was there had been a huge smoke in the sky at the time and his entire race avoided this place until it started to cool. Nevertheless, crossing the black wasteland is the only way we can reach the others at the great denzel gathering. Alheeza lowered his head, focusing on the ground ahead as he pressed on.*

Amanda whipped an arm across her sweating forehead. Looking around at the dark wasteland, she mind-spoke: Nothing could live here!

*We are here, are we not?* replied Alheeza.

*Not for long I hope!*

Jamie unslung his drink bottle as he strode after the other two. His thirst was raging in the heat. "Wait you two, I am overdressed." His thick hair hung in clumps that stuck to his cheeks and neck. Sliding his gear to the ground, he neatly stacked his spear and flinger alongside it. He quickly rolled up the sleeves and legs of his jump suit, as well as opening it to his naval. For a moment he stared at the crystal that hung in its neat sling, about his neck. "I wonder who designed these suits? They're cold at night and hot in the day! I think I could have done better" he muttered to himself.

"I know I could have!" said Amanda.

As Jamie looked up, he could see that she had peeled back her jumpsuit back as well. It was not high fashion, but she looked great with slim legs and forearms. Gone was her sickly pale skin from weeks ago. The neck seal was also opened half way down her chest glistening with perspiration. Trying not to stare, he took in the small breasts that pressed against the thin material.

Jamie's attention shifted as Amanda said, "I don't know how much more of this heat I can take!"

Looking up at the sun, Jamie said, "Me either, and we haven't even reached the full heat of the day." Moving into mind-speak, he added: *Alheeza, we are using more water than I expected. Will we make it across soon?*

*I am not sure of our exact arrival. All we can do is press on.*

*Somehow I knew that was the answer,* mind-spoke Amanda.

---

The smooth ridge seemed to climb slowly on forever. Amanda felt herself being driven mad from the oppressive heat. Alheeza was sprinting on ahead. *What do you see?* she mind-spoke.

Their denzel friend did not reply; instead, he kept up his pace until he reached the summit. He looked each way as if trying to decide which way to go. The two humans finally caught up with him, gazing out upon the vast wasteland.

"Oh crap, it goes on for ever! It's like the mountains are no closer!" exclaimed Amanda.

*I am afraid my memories of this area are incomplete. I believe I have underestimated our ability to cross this in a day.*

"No shit!" added Jamie.

*That does not translate,* mind-spoke Alheeza.

*It means I cannot believe my eyes. Also, I am deeply disappointed.*

131

"No shit!" added Amanda.

Jamie shook his empty water container. *And this could mean disaster.*

*The outcome does not look promising,* telepathed Alheeza.

*There is nothing for it but to press on, is there?* telepathed Amanda, looking from one to the other.

*I am afraid not.*

---

It had been almost two hours since they had left the summit, their feet dragged with fatigue and their mouths were so dry that swallowing was impossible.

All about them, the glassy black hills shimmered in the rising heat waves. Everything looked distorted as if their very minds were drying in the insufferable heat. Alheeza felt a crippling doubt about their ability to survive the passage. How had he come to this void in his memories without some sort of alarm? The Valley of Desolation deserved its name in every way.

Jamie called a halt. He squatted to apply copeander to another cut on his foot. As Amanda came up beside him, he could see her feet were suffering as well. Pulling out his drinking bottle, he tipped the last few drops into his mouth. It was not enough to even swallow. He mind-spoke: *That is it then, we have no more water. How much farther Alheeza?*

*Too far. I have failed you.*

*I have never heard you despondent before,* mind-spoke Jamie.

Amanda's face said it all, fear was traced across it as she looked from Jamie to Alheeza, and then into the distance.

They were standing in a small gulley, shuffling from foot to foot when Jamie noticed something peculiar farther down the gulley. *Alheeza is that a hole over there?*

As they approached the shadow it revealed itself to be an opening in the smooth black stone. It was about twice as long as Jamie was tall and about half that wide. Jamie crouched down to peer within, but it was difficult to see details with the bright sun behind him. He lay down his things, using their sleeping roll to protect himself, as he lay prone, trying to look at the opening.

"Amanda, I could lower you down on my rope, so you can have a look around." He said over his shoulder. "I don't think it is all that deep."

"Sure, anything to get out of the heat!"

It didn't take long to tie a knot in the rope to pass a sling under her arms. Carefully, she crouched at the edge of the opening. Jamie took up the slack on the line as she slid over the edge. She did not drop far before the resistance lessened, and within two more arm lengths of rope, she reached the bottom.

"What's it like?"

*Just give me a moment for my eyes to adjust.*

Jamie and Alheeza exchanged glances before she continued.

*It seems to be a long smooth tunnel. Wait a minute, there is something shiny ahead.*

They could hear her footsteps on the hard surface.

*You're not going to believe this, but there is water laying in a low part of the tunnel.*

*Is it clean water?* mind-spoke Alheeza.

*It smells a bit of sulfur. I am not sure if it is good enough to drink.*

Jamie looked at Alheeza. *Should we go down there to check it out?*

*Perhaps, but how do I get down there?* telepathed Alheeza.

*I will lower you, just like I did with Amanda.*

*And what about you? How will you get down without help, not to mention how do we get back up?*

*Well, the way I see it is this, if we do not take shelter down there, we will cook up here. I think we have to take the risk. I might be able to climb up that wall but first, we need to get out of this heat before it kills us.*

Alheeza squinted into the intense sun, still tracking high in the sky, and then back to Jamie, mind-speaking: *This is not how our race would undertake the problem, but I fear my inexperience has led us to this dilemma. Your choice might be the best solution.*

*Do not be so hard on yourself; we have made a good team so far.*

Without further debate, the young denzel allowed himself to be lowered through the gash in the rock.

Jamie handed his things down to them on a rope. Then he slid carefully backwards over the ledge. Just as he thought it was all going so well, he lost his grip on the serrated stone. His fingers stung as he plummeted into the darkness. At first, it felt as if he would fall forever, but then he was sliding against the curved wall. He didn't stop until he had slid part way up the other side and then back to the middle. Jamie came to rest on his back, looking up through the hole which he had just plummeted from.

Ah, that smarts! he mind-spoke, as he looked at his scratched finger tips. Small droplets of blood were just forming as he watched.

"Let me see," said Amanda as she crouched to look at his hands. "I guess it is my turn to tend to your wounds."

"Yeah, I guess so."

Digging into the side of his pack, she drew some of the healing fruit. "We don't have much of this left. Will we be able to get any more of it later?"

*I assure you that the forest on the other side of the Grey Mountains has this healing fruit,* telepathed Alheeza.

*Good, we always seem to need it,* she replied.

As Amanda set about dabbing his fingers with the astringent, Jamie took in their surroundings for the first time. It was like some great worm had eaten a path through the solid rock. He shivered at the thought of a creature doing something like that.

When she had finished Jamie looked up and down the dark shaft: *What made this tunnel, Alheeza?*

*I do not know.*

*I wish we had more light to see what is down here,* mind-spoke Amanda.

Instinctively Jamie pulled his ruby crystal from his jump-suit. At first, it was just barely a glow, a mere red glitter. Whether it was the faint glow of the ruby stone or his enhanced senses when he made contact, Jamie didn't know, but he was soon able to make out more details down the tunnel. He could see the fine, smooth ripples that formed concentric rings all along the corridor. He slid his hand along the polished surface, mind-speaking: *I wonder how far this thing goes?*

Amanda looked back over her shoulder before telepathing: *And where did it come from?*

*I do not believe our race has ever seen this.*

*And how do we get back out?* added Amanda.

Walking back to the opening, Jamie stared up into the brightness.

As Amanda came to stand next to him she said, "What if I get on your shoulders, I might be able to reach the edge."

*But how do you get a grip to pull yourself out?* mind-spoke Jamie.

Nobody answered him, they just looked up.

*I think we should rest before making any more decisions,* added Alheeza.

*Makes sense to me!* telepathed Amanda. *At least we are not cooking in that unforgiving sun!*

*Is that water drinkable, Alheeza?* mind-spoke Jamie.

Alheeza padded over to the shallow pool. Cautiously, he tasted the water. Slowly, he turned back to them. *A mouthful or two, but it might make you sick if you have more.*

"That is better than nothing!" mumbled Amanda.

She bent to the glistening pool, dipping her cupped hand into the cool water. It tasted bitter but her mouth felt so much better after the scorching heat. She splashed her face several times and then her jump-suit. "Oh, that feels better!" she said.

Jamie followed her example and found the pool refreshing even though it did smell a bit off.

Alheeza mind-spoke: *What are our choices now?*

Amanda looked from one to the other before adding: *Why not follow the tunnel?*

*Alheeza, do you have any sense of direction down here?* Jamie asked.

*I believe so.*

*What if this tunnel could lead us out of here?*

*Again, it is not in the nature of our race to travel an uncharted path, but given our circumstances, I believe we have little choice.*

*All right then, let us see if we can find another opening,* mind-spoke Jamie.

Jamie splashed through the shallow pool, his silhouette clearly visible from his glowing crystal.

---

Without the sun tracking overhead, Jamie lost track of time passing. The tunnel they followed seemed to bore a hole through the solid black rock. It curved from side to side as if seeking the easiest way forward. In the low areas, they splashed through shallow puddles of water; at one point the water was almost waist deep before it rose again to a dry level. Alheeza took these wet patches with ease, swimming in the deepest one with his narrow head held high. It was Amanda who became more and more agitated the farther they went into the darkness. The dim red glow of Jamie's precious gem reflected off the smooth interior like some melted mirror. Time seemed to drag in the endless night of their subterranean passage. Several times she took out her own amber stone hoping for more illumination, but it remained dark. The punishing heat above ground was long forgotten, for it was now replaced with a foreboding.

*How much longer can this thing go on, and why has there been no other opening to the surface?* mind-spoke Amanda.

*You know that none of us has that knowledge,* telepathed Alheeza.

"Of course, I know that! I just feel like this tunnel is starting to close in on me! I really need to get out of here!" Amanda said through gritted teeth.

*Wait, what is that noise?* mind-spoke Jamie.

Everyone turned to gaze back from where they had come. At first, Amanda could hear nothing, but then a distant rumbling echoed down the tube.

"Run, everybody run!" shouted Jamie.

As one, they turned to flee down the passage.

"What is it?" screamed Amanda.

*Water! A great deal of water is coming.*

Jamie ran like he had never run before, heedless of the flapping pack and its assorted attachments. The silhouettes of his running companions were outlined from the dim light cast by his tightly clasped crystal. Then the thundering grew from a distant rumble to a deafening roar, just before the cascading wall hit. Somehow Jamie got a last breath before the chaos of churning black water tumbled him head over heels. In the confusion, there was no air, no up, no down, only a rising panic that this was the end. He felt his eyes bulge as his body screamed for a breath of air. Just when he was sure all hope was gone, he felt the weightlessness of freefall as the water was torn apart by rushing air. Somehow he gulped in more air than water just as his body was smashed into solid water. He drifted freely in his dark watery grave. Panic was replaced by calm. His vision started to darken around the edges as he stared at the glow of his ruby crystal, while it drifted up in front of his face. Somehow he knew he was about to breathe in a lung full of water. There was nothing he could do about it. His arm was jerked painfully upward as his face was thrust above the surface. He gasped for life-giving air, sputtering and gasping again. Instinctively, he thrashed at the water trying to stay on the surface.

*Stop fighting! I cannot hold you up if you struggle,* came Amanda's thought signature.

He tried to relax, but the panic kept bubbling up through the terror of deep water in the dark.

*I am at your side also. Calm yourself, or you will kill us all!* mind-spoke Alheeza with a type of authority that he had not sensed before.

Relax, he could not do, but he could go rigid. Gulping in grateful lungs full of air, Jamie started to take in his surroundings. Somewhere in the darkness, water thundered, not unlike the waterfall. It was night, with the stars reflecting off the rippling water. A sliver of a moon defined the palisade of rising rock. Part way up the cliff, starlight sparkled off the spout of water disgorging from the tunnel.

Amanda's mind-speech interrupted him: *You never learned to swim, did you?*

He felt something else under his arm, and Alheeza's head appeared next to him.

*Grasp me around the neck and we will swim you ashore, my friend.*

Unable to think of anything to say, Jamie just let them drag him to shore.

Sharp rocks cut into his knees as he crawled up the shore. Something clattered beside him and it was the first time he realized that he still had hold of his spear and flinger.

"You can't swim, but you never lose track of your spear! You really are something, Jamie Chambers," panted Amanda.

Jamie couldn't believe how heavy he felt as he struggled from the water's edge. His thin jump-suit streamed water as he staggered amongst the jagged rocks. Collapsing on a narrow patch of gravel, he took in his surroundings. By the starlight, he could just make out a sizable lake, with hills climbing steeply all around. Where had the other two gone?

"What are you two up to?" he called.

"Alheeza is helping me collect our things, at least the ones that still float," Amanda called back.

Not long afterwards the other two joined him, dripping onto the gravel. Amanda took in Jamie, shivering in his damp clothing. She mind-spoke: *I think you are going into shock. We need to get you warm again. Alheeza, what are the options for shelter?*

*There appears to be an overhang in the boulders over there, at least we will have protection from the breeze and from eyes above.*

Amanda ushered Jamie into the shadows of the leaning rocks. It was not Sanctuary, but she thought it would do for the night. She moved as quickly as she could to shake as much water as she could out of the coarse sleeping blanket. Then she set about stabilizing Jamie.

# Sharp Stones

amie struggled in the black depths of the water not knowing up from down, his lungs were about to burst. His eyes fluttered open to reveal jagged mountains painted in the morning sunlight. The terror of the dream faded slowly as Amanda squeezed his shoulder. Slowly, he took in his surroundings, like he had never seen them before. Alheeza was curled up with his back to Jamie's chest, with the faint but distinct odor of his other-world friend filling his nostrils. It was the arms around his bare chest that felt the best. He was just starting to assess his state of dress, or more to the point, his state of undress when Amanda whispered, "You're awake."

Jamie could feel her face pressed into his back. He struggled, trying to think of what to say next. Finally he said in a low voice, "Thank you for saving me."

He could feel her warm tears trickling down his back. "I don't know what I would do if I lost you too."

He was about to roll over when she flung back the edge of the blanket, jumping up. With her back to him she pulled on a damp jump-suit from a nearby rock. She turned, looking down at him. "Don't you ever scare me like that again!"

His momentary excitement at seeing her dress vanished in her burst of anger.

"I didn't try to drown you!" he said a little more forcefully than he meant.

Sniffing, she turned to walk down to the beach. Kneeling, Amanda started to pick through their salvaged gear.

Alheeza mind-spoke: *You are not of my race, but let me say this, when your mate is angry, find a way to make peace.*

"When did you become a psychologist?" Jamie blurted out. "And any way, she is not my mate. We are just friends."

*Your words do not always translate, but you are a mating pair. That is all that is important. She is bonded to you and you are bonded to her. A mating pair, yes?*

Jamie just stared out at Amanda. What he felt for this tough, young woman, he could not put into words. She was the most important person alive to him.

He rose, pulling on a damp garment. It stuck to his skin as he walked down to the beach. Amanda was setting out clumps of Herman nuts to dry in the sun. Squatting down, he put a hand on her arm. As their eyes met, he heard himself say, "I have never loved like I love you. To be parted from you would tear my heart out."

Blinking away the tears, she said, "Now why couldn't you say that before?"

She reached up and they clung to each other for what seemed an eternity.

---

Standing on top of a jagged boulder, Jamie surveyed the surrounding area. He and Amanda had been exploring along the rugged shoreline, waiting for their salvaged supplies to dry in the sun. He could hear Amanda scrambling up behind him.

"It looks like that mass of smooth black rock that we crossed must have flowed down the wide valley, like some thick liquid. Doesn't that make it volcanic in its origin?" Jamie said.

"You are more of the geologist than I, but it really does look like it just flowed along like half-melted ice cream."

They stood on their small vantage point, taking in their surroundings. The lake must have been 10 kilometers long and half that wide. All around it was a palisade of boulders. On the other side it gave way to foothills that appeared to have the first real vegetation they had seen since leaving Sanctuary. Beyond that, the grey mountains rose high above them with flecks of white hinting at last winter's snow. There was no apparent valley leading beyond.

"Alheeza said that if we pick our way along this shore, we can make our way into the mountains. He has regained his bearings and remembers a narrow pass."

Amanda had not answered him, and as he turned he could see her looking over the edge of their boulder. "What do you see?" he asked.

"I'm not sure, but come here and have a look!"

Getting down on his hands and knees, Jamie peered over the edge. In the shadow he could see a black rock that had been ground between the boulders. Shards of glistening stone were strewn along the edge. A feeling of excitement surged through him as he scrambled down to explore the narrow slot with Amanda following behind.

Jamie squatted by the shattered stone, idly picking up a piece. "Crap! This is really sharp," he muttered sucking his thumb. Amanda looked first at the black sliver of stone and then at his thumb. As he drew it from his mouth, she could see a clean slice along the tip of it.

"What is it?" she asked.

"The sharpest thing I've ever seen in my life!" replied Jamie. He held up the small object, "Look!"

In the shadow, she could see a slender sliver of what appeared to be, black glass. "OK, so it's really sharp, but does it break easily?"

Carefully holding the blunt, wide edge, Jamie experimentally, tapped the sharp side on a larger stone. It rang a tiny high note but did not break. He continued to tap more vigorously, and the slender blade finally shattered. "OK, that was a whole lot tougher than I thought a piece of glass could be. All I can guess is that this is not your ordinary glass."

"This could be useful, couldn't it?" asked Amanda.

"Oh, yes! This is going to be very useful indeed," he said as he started collecting promising shards. They returned to their camp full of excitement.

*Alheeza, you have to see what we found!* Jamie announced as they picked their way towards him holding their flat rock trays arrayed with various glass shards.

After the excitement of finding the sharp stone, Alheeza led them along the shore where the boulders finally gave way to a narrow washed pebble beach. He assured them that later that day they would have a most satisfactory campsite.

As they followed their denzel friend, the two humans discussed how to prepare for the journey ahead. Amanda's shoes had some deep cuts that were tearing along the seams. Experimentally, she walked bare foot for a while on the washed gravel.

Amanda mind-spoke: *I am amazed at how your feet toughened up back at Sanctuary, but what will you do if it starts to get really cold when we climb near those snow-covered mountains?*

*I do not really know. I was hoping you would come up with some extraordinary solution from the plants we find.*

*That is a bit like believing in magic, don't you think?*

*The weavings that you did back at the cave were remarkable.*

*It is kind of you to say that, but they are pretty crude compared to the fine material that our jump suits are made of. And that is without trying to figure out how to protect my feet. I do not have a month to toughen up before we climb more rocky trails.*

Alheeza interrupted: *I have a question.*

*Go on, what is your question?* telepathed Amanda.

*From my observations, you appear to suffer in these outer skins when it is hot and yet when it is cold they do not seem to keep you warm enough. Much of the time I cannot see why you wear them at all?*

*Modesty.*

Alheeza turned to look at Amanda: *The more time we spend together the better I understand you, but what is this modesty?*

*We cover our bodies so that our sexual attraction is reduced. It helps when our people lived in very close contact with each other. Disputes and rivalry are defused. Also by using color, we stand apart from our peers.*

*How does this modesty apply when there are just the two of you? This morning, both of you covered your nakedness by putting on wet clothing that made you visibly more chilled. What was the point? There are no others here to see you.*

Amanda nodded: *All right, you have me there. I would have been warmer without my damp jump-suit, but still Jamie and I are uninitiated. We have not, how shall I put this? We have not reached a point where we have started to plant the seeds of our future offspring.*

*Oh, your mating is not complete!*

Through all of this Jamie looked decidedly uncomfortable. How did Amanda know all these things? What he felt was a mixture of excitement mixed with bewilderment?

*If we are having this frank conversation, I have some questions too.* mind-spoke Amanda.

*I am open to questions.*

*At what age do you mate in your race?*

*I have to reach full maturity first, that will take another 40 of our full season cycles.*

*You have to be 55 years old before you can take a mate and have offspring?*

*That is approximately correct.*

*But that would make you 110 before you would see your next generation, we call them grandchildren.*

*If I am lucky and the Great Raptors do not intervene, I may see several generations.*

Amanda's mouth dropped open at the revelation.

---

Alheeza was back in his element. Not long before nightfall, he led them around the lake and up into the foothills. There in a narrow ravine, a thick rock lintel created a roof over a deep recess. Wanting to experiment with the new sharp stones, Jamie quickly removed one of the large black flakes. Gripping it with part of his old shoe, he set off to collect tinder. In no time, he had a pile of dried limbs cut from the scrub brush that lined the ravine. Amanda stripped young branches heavy in leaf, to make a bed for them at the back of the recess. As darkness closed in around them, flames rose from their fire to paint dancing images on the underside of the overhanging rock. Nestling into the comfort of their natural bed, they took their meal of nuts and dried fruit.

Amanda opened Jamie's old survival book to reread the sections on primitive foot wear and warm clothing. "Jamie," she said, "most of the stuff in this book assumes that we are a hunting party with readily available tanned hides."

*What is this tanned hide you refer to?* inserted Alheeza.

*Our ancestors killed animals and then treated their hides so that they stayed soft and did not rot. Also, the animals on our planet had fur, you know like the hair on our heads but it is all over their bodies. There is no equivalent for that here.*

*You need some skin that has a fluffy covering. One that is soft and flexible.*

*And it has to be big enough to cut out large sections as wide as this.* Amanda held out her hands to indicate about a meter wide.

*Could it be from a plant?*

*I never thought of that, but I suppose it could.*

*In the morning we will go off our trail to visit a stand of special plants.*

She crawled into the fold of the sleeping rug, where she fell instantly asleep.

Jamie had his collection of glass shards spread out in front of him. There were a variety of shapes and sizes, and all had at least one very sharp edge. He dragged his ironwood spear over to examine the point. It had blunted with use and could hardly be called pointed, especially after seeing these razor-sharp stones. He flicked through his great-grandfather's book, looking for clues to attach a blade to the end of a shaft. He knew that he had a solution close at hand, but couldn't quite resolve how to do it.

Alheeza, always curious about Jamie's tools, watched fascinated.

*I am sure you can see all of that, but it is still just a stick to me.*

Their heads turned in unison as a distant Raptor call reached them. Jamie tossed a branch on the fire, before stepping out into the ravine. With the fire behind him, he clasped his crystal to see better into the night sky. Above their narrow valley, nothing moved. Still feeling edgy, Jamie went back to the fire. He sat up for some time feeding twigs onto their fire. Every so often he would step out from under the rock ledge to scan the sky, but no sign of the night raider was seen or heard again.

There was something farther up the valley, a large creature on four legs that looked at him with pale red eyes. After a few moments, it retreated. The sight of it made his skin crawl, but there seemed nothing to do about it, at least for now.

In the glow of the fire, he was able to deepen the groove on his unfinished flinger. Using a small glass shard carefully clasped in a section of his shoe, made an ideal carving tool. He still hadn't worked out all the details of this contraption, but he was hopeful. A stronger length of red elastic sap was his next modification. Drawing it back along its length he could feel the increasing tension. This would be much better than his failed bows. Unable to solve the trigger, he set it aside and picked up his spear. Experimentally, he checked the fire-hardened tip. His knife barely scraped the surface, but plainly it was a dull point compared with his collection of glass shards. On impulse he flipped the spear over, testing the unburned part of the shaft. It was still workable, so he set about cutting a slot for one of the glass shards.

Amanda crawled out of her bed sometime later, asking sleepily why he was still up.

Jamie mind-spoke: *I heard a Raptor. I could not sleep, so I was fitting a glass shard into the tip of my spear while I kept the fire going.*

*Let me tend the fire and you get some sleep, OK?*

It did not take long before his rhythmic breathing came from the sleeping rug.

In the predawn light, he crawled out, gave her a hug and ushered her back to their bed.

# If the Shoe Fits

———————◇———————

Amanda was in Jamie's tight embrace, her hand slid down his naked back, and over the tight muscles of his buttocks. He was whispering something in her ear as her eyes fluttered open. Faint impressions of a mind-speak conversation drifted to her. As images came into focus, she could see Jamie and Alheeza huddled together out in the sunlight. The last shreds of her dream evaporated, allowing the morning chill to penetrate her reality. She sat up stiffly, looking around. A shiver ran up her back as she stretched her cold limbs.

*I didn't know you could whisper in mind-speak,* she interjected.

They both turned to look at her.

"We didn't want to wake you, that's all," said Jamie.

*What's going on?*

Alheeza mind-spoke: *Again the complexities of Jamie's tools challenge me. As best I can understand, he needs some sticky material that will hold one of his sharp stones on the end of a stick. Then it has to harden. I am presently searching my memory for a clue to this problem.*

Amanda was about to ask a question when Alheeza continued.

*Later this morning I will lead you to the jb—na-heea growth.*

The plant name did not translate, but she knew it was something to do with her leather substitutes.

———————◇———————

Amanda followed the other two as they picked their way over exposed hills and through the dense bush of the hollows. Her mind wandered as she watched the feet of her companion, wondering how she would solve the problem of their deteriorating clothing. As

146

if coming out of a dream, she realized she was walking in shadows. They had come to a completely new type of forest. The spindly stocks of the serrated-leaf brush had changed abruptly. Instead, trees with enormous yellow trunks reached up to vast domed tops from which thin brown sheets were hanging and rippling in the breeze.

Alheeza had stopped to look up as he mind-spoke: *This is the jb—na-heea. It grows only in valleys such as this. We were lucky to be nearby when you made your request.*

*How do we use it?* telepathed Jamie.

*This has many of the properties for making clothing that Amanda asked for. How to collect it is not part of our memories, we only observe and remember. That is how we survive. Knowledge is everything. Tools and devices are from your world, not ours.*

Jamie looked up at the giant plant. It was unlike anything he had seen so far. Large enough at its base that the trunk must have been two meters through, and too tall to judge. As he prodded the surface of what he thought was bark, he found it was covered in a thick layer of soft fine hairs. When he pulled on the thin filaments they were surprisingly tough.

*How could we use this stuff?*

As he pondered, he heard a shout from deep in the forest. Following Amanda's voice he came to a toppled giant that had crushed on two smaller ones.

"Look at this Jamie." Amanda was fingering the sheets on the underside of the domed top. "It is really quite flexible. I tried ripping it with my hand and it won't budge. What do you think?"

Jamie took out his knife and sawed off a section. Experimentally he pulled it and then tried to tear it. He could cut it easily, but he couldn't make it rip. Handing it back to Amanda, he walked to the base where it had broken free of its roots. The hairy bark was shredded where the trunk had failed. Grabbing the edge, he tried to tear a section free but found it surprisingly tough. He poked at the spongy inner core, unsure of what use it would be. Using his knife he tried cutting through the outer section, only to find the hairy surface seemed to impede his blade. When he slipped the knife under the edge, it cut quite easily. Slicing a long section, he carefully peeled the soft bark back. He felt Amanda at his side, and said, "What do you think of this?"

She ran her hand along the surface and then along the underside. A smile slowly spread across her face. "I think Alheeza is a genius!"

"So do I!"

*Do I sense praise being sent my way?* came Alheeza's response.

Quickly, Jamie and Amanda collected several sections of bark as well as two sheets from under the dome. With their prizes carefully rolled and slung over their shoulders, they set off with Alheeza to look for the next camp.

---

They followed Alheeza farther up the valley, barely noticing that the forest was changing all around them. While they walked among trees that dwarfed the carpet domes, Amanda talked excitedly about their new find. Since *jb—na-heea* failed to translate, they decided to call them "carpet domes". And then Alheeza led them to a huge tree with multiple roots that rose high out of the ground to form a single tall tree with a tuft of turquoise foliage far above.

*It is beautiful,* mind-spoke Amanda.

The lithe denzel threaded his way through the massive roots to a mound of packed earth within. As Jamie and Amanda followed, pushing their gear ahead of them, they were amazed again at the resourcefulness of their guide.

While Jamie looked about the palisade of thick roots, he mind-spoke: *This looks completely Raptor proof.*

*My race have used these for generations on their way to the gathering.*

*Last night I saw another large creature up the trail, but it turned away, and I did not see it again.*

*That was,* and here Alheeza paused trying to translate the name, *from our conversation about your Earth history, let us call it a mountain-wolf. That is as close as we need to be. It lives in these high lands and is a predator of considerable stature. They will become more numerous as we approach the gathering. Usually, they are not a problem for a family unit, but to a lone traveler, they can be dangerous.*

Jamie was looking around the space. The inside of the roots circle with a very high ceiling was about 10 meters across. As he stared, he thought he could see light from somewhere above, but it was not clear. Later that night, the hollow trunk turned out to be a natural chimney that drew the smoke from their fire out through an unseen hole.

After their evening meal, Amanda unrolled a section of the hairy bark and began scraping it with one of the glass wedges. Before long, she had a section of very pliable material.

Losing interest, Alheeza soon curled up by the fire and went to sleep. Jamie pulled out the rest of his glass shards and set about working on the spear. He and Amanda talked in whispered voices as they set about their tasks. She stopped scraping and looked at Jamie's callused and scarred foot. She fetched a piece of charcoal from the fire and kneeled by Jamie with a section of the brown leaf material. "Hold still while I trace your foot." she said.

Just the touch of her hand on his foot set off a chain reaction within. She was so intent on her work that she did not notice the flush that came to Jamie's face and how his breathing picked up. He was just reaching to run his hand along her long neck, when she pulled the material from under his foot, tossed it aside, and returned to her scraping. When she had finished her first section of bark, she held it up for inspection, saying, "I like this stuff. We can make all kinds of things from it."

Jamie reached over to feel the hairy bark. "It sure is softer than your first rug. Not that I am complaining, because that rug is way warmer than sleeping in the open. But this will be even better."

She smiled broadly at him. Without thinking, he stroked her cheek. "You're amazing, you know."

She drew him close, kissing him on the lips. Who made the next move was never clear, but the feeling of their bodies pressed against each other set a fire within each of them that left them panting and flushed.

Amanda sat back on her heals, running her fingers through her tussled hair saying, "That was nice."

Jamie blushed, unable to find any words to fill the gap, so Amanda came to his rescue by saying, "I want to finish scraping these sections before turning in."

"I have things to finish too," he said, but in his heart all he wanted to do was touch her again. Touch her all over.

Using all of his will power, he picked up his projectile device and set about experimenting with a simple trigger that could release one of his arrows.

# An Unwelcome Guest

---

The air had a crisp edge to it that morning as the trio penetrated ever farther through this strange land. The conversation was sparse as Jamie and Amanda followed Alheeza along the twisting trail through the forest. There were glimpses of the high mountains ahead, but they seemed no closer today than the day before. Jamie was admiring the sap that Alheeza had found for him in the afternoon and noticing how it glistened on the tightly-wrapped binding of his glass spear point.

Alheeza mind-spoke, *We must make haste to reach our next safe campsite.*

They had not been on the trail for long, and Jamie was trying to adjust his heavy pack to reduce the chaff, when Alheeza froze on the trail in front of him.

*What is it my friend?* telepathed Jamie.

*I sense a mountain-wolf nearby. We must take care because they can attack without warning.*

Jamie shuddered as he looked about. *How can you tell?*

*They have a foul smell, not unlike a Great Raptor, but not as strong. Do you not smell it?*

*No, I believe your sense of smell is far more sensitive.*

Amanda edged up beside Jamie: *What should I do?*

*Drop your pack and get your spear ready.*

They stood close to each other, the humans trying hard not to make any noise. Bushes twitched ahead on the trail as the stocky predator stepped into view some distance up the path. Jamie had not seen one of these creatures up close before and was stunned at how malevolent it looked. Sliding his pack to the ground, he took a firm grip of his spear. The black glass shard glinted in the late afternoon sun. Alheeza was in a guarded crouch with the scales on his back lifting. Over Amanda's rapid breathing, Jamie felt a cold shiver of fear trickle down his spine.

*What does your race do when facing one of these animals?* Jamie mind-spoke.

*We usually avoid confrontations by traveling in larger groups. The three of us are too few to threaten it.*

Looking past Jamie, Amanda sized up the mountain-wolf. Twice the size of a wilda-cat, it had dark, heavy plates of scales over its shoulders and a pale yellow underside. Although it lacked the thick chest of the cats, its wide head with powerful jaws agape gave her a chill. It was looking straight at her with intense red eyes, its yellow tongue salivating between sharp teeth.

The creature climbed to the higher side of the trail as if assessing the best way to attack.

Jamie stepped beside Alheeza mind-speaking: *If it comes at us suddenly, step quickly to the left and just before it reaches us, step just as quickly back beside me. I'll do the rest.* He hoped that he sounded more confident than he felt, but it was the best plan he could come up with.

*I will trust you know what you are about.*

Amanda was taking big gulps of air as she kept moving to put Jamie between her and the approaching mountain-wolf. She had been cold before, but now sweat was beading on her forehead.

Almost without thinking, Jamie drew out his crystal, feeling not only the enhanced senses that it gave him but also a calmness that allowed him to truly see his opponent just as the creature leapt forward. Jamie grasped the spear in both hands, crouching for the impact. With surprising speed the mountain-wolf closed the gap. Jamie saw peripherally Alheeza springing to the left and then bound back while sensing the wolf's momentary distraction. He jabbed the shaft forward, the impact sending a terrible jolt up into his arms driving him backward, his feet skidding on the gravel. The shaft of his spear twisted as the predator hit the ground beside him.

The mountain wolf was on its side snapping viciously at thin air.

Jamie pulled his spear free and, hoisting high above his head, he drove it into the side of the writhing creature. Its screams echoed through the hills as Amanda thrust her own spear into the throat of the thrashing beast. It jerked several times and then lay still. The quiet that followed seemed unnatural.

The three survivors stared down at the prone attacker, dark blood oozing from its many wounds.

*I would not call that a clean kill by any means,* mind-spoke Jamie.

*I would argue otherwise,* telepathed Alheeza.

Jamie rolled the carcass over to examine his first spear thrust. What he saw made his breath catch. He had been hoping to spear the creature in the chest as he had done with the wilda-cat, but it had been moving so fast that his thrust was more of a guess. His weapon had caught the creature in the shoulder where the razor sharp tip had slid under its protective scales, ripping it open two thirds of the way along its side. It must have severed some of the front leg muscles causing the wolf to collapse. It probably would have bled to death had they not quickened the process by stabbing it again.

Amanda wrinkled her nose at the perfidious odour that arose from the carcass. *Better it than us, is all I can say.*

*You have defended us in a most gallant way,* telepathed Alheeza.

*I did not know you understood the meaning of gallant?* answered Jamie.

*I have been in your company for some time and our cultures have blurred somewhat.*

# The Mountain That Moves

A ll morning, they passed through the tall forest, stopping only to collect more fruit and nuts. When they chanced upon a copeander tree, they collected more of the medicinal fruit. The valley rose into rugged foot hills, and as they climbed they left the last of the giant trees behind. Amanda had been daydreaming about the previous night's fondling with giggles and kisses, when they emerged into bright sunlight, she looked up. The mountains that had always seemed close, now stood before her. Their grey crags rose in pyramid fashion to form a palisade of solid rock far above them. A tumbling river emerged from a deep wedge that cut through the stone barricade not far ahead.

Shrieks from above made Amanda look up into the blue sky, where a large triangular flying creature circled, making her shudder.

Jamie, seeing the terror etched across her face, leaned forward saying, "They are not Great Raptors, remember they only come out at night. These are far too small, maybe a meter or two across at most."

"How did you know what I was thinking?" asked Amanda.

"Your feelings are written all over your face."

*Now who is practicing psychology?*

Jamie gave her one of his lopsided grins and turned to follow Alheeza who had started down the trail ahead of them.

Alheeza mind-spoke: *We must get up that valley before nightfall, because it gets dark sooner there.*

The hike was easier going downhill, but it was farther to the river than it looked. It was almost an hour before they crunched along in the gravel next to the rapidly flowing water.

The steep valley zig-zagged through the massive mountains, and Amanda felt the first chill as the deep shadows enfolded them. Amanda tucked one arm into her rough vest trying to conserve heat.

Alheeza led them to a place where the river had undercut the canyon wall, revealing a collapsed stone. The space beneath the lintel formed a natural cave with a small opening at one end and a larger one at the other.

*How long until dark Alheeza? Jamie telepathed.*

*In your time, about an hour.*

Dropping his gear, Jamie looked up and down the valley before adding: *I had better start gathering tonight's fire wood.* To himself, he muttered, "And by the look of this valley, firewood is going to get harder to find."

Amanda mind-spoke: *All right, I want to start planning how I can make us some warm clothing from our carpet dome bark.*


While the humans set about their tasks, Alheeza strolled up the trail until he was looking at the steep cliff that rose above the valley. The late afternoon sun was painting the uppermost section in golden light. It should have been a tranquil scene, but a slight shiver ran over his scales as a vague sense of foreboding crept up his back.

He looked back at the spiral of smoke rising from his alien friends' fire. He could see them crouching over their tools and crafts. Their magic with those things still fascinated and eluded him all at the same time. With an almost human shrug, he turned to pad up the valley to see if there were dark combs that grew from dead shrubs. He salivated at the thought of these tasty treats. He might even bring a few back to see if the humans would like them.

Alheeza was returning with several large wedges of dark comb in his mouth when his scales stood on end as a shudder ran down his spine. He looked up at the steep mountain face before him, its upper cliff now in shadow. His foreboding intensified and then he felt the first of the ground tremors he'd been anticipating. As the shaking stopped, he looked down the trail barely making out the wisps of smoke from their camp. The ground heaved again, this time making him stagger and in that moment he knew he would surely die unless he found safer ground. Alheeza turned, his legs a blur as he sped back up the trail. Behind him, the mountain roared.

---

Next to their crackling fire, Jamie was enjoying the feel of Amanda's slender muscular body pressed against his when the first tremor hit. Not knowing why, he spun to look up at the vast wedge of rock that formed the mountain face just beyond them. The ground heaved again, making them both reach out to catch their balance. Far above, the great cliff seemed to shift, crumbling before his eyes, accelerating at an amazing speed. Dust rose in billowing clouds hiding the cascading rock, lightning flashing within. The earth shook as the avalanche of rock careened towards them. Time stood still, but somehow Jamie scooped up his weapons and grabbed Amanda's hand, dragging her under the rock refuge.

The great slab of rock that sheltered them quivered and dust fell from the surface as everything shook. Outside, day turned to night as the deafening roar intensified. Something heavy thudded on the lintel above while everything was filled with choking dust. The crashing and banging intensified, and suddenly ceased as a great quiet spread across the valley.

Jamie thought he heard Amanda whimpering, until he realized it was him. He could feel her quivering body held tightly against his chest. Rock dust burned his eyes as he tried to look about in the darkness. He pulled the edge of his jump-suit up trying to filter out the dust, but only managed to cough more from the dirt clinging to it. Gathering as much strength as he could, he said, "We're still alive."

# The Phoenix

W ere they entombed within a rocky grave? Jamie could feel a rising panic within as he groped in the dust-filled darkness to make sense of his surroundings. Time dragged until the dust settled and he could make out a dim triangle of light near the entrance.

"Do you see the light? I have to see if we can get out of here," Jamie whispered, his words seeming louder in the silence.

Crawling on his hands and knees, he worked his way past their scattered supplies to the entrance. A large rock blocked most of the exit, but he could see a light patch of sky showing through the gray rock dust. "We can get out!" he called back to Amanda.

"Oh Jamie, are you sure?"

After he clambered through the slot between the boulders, he took in the valley below. The dust cloud was being carried up the valley on a light breeze revealing the full extent of the rock flow. Just a short time before, a small river was flowing freely down the slope. Now boulders the size of storage bays on the Mayflower were heaped one on top of the other, creating a massive pile of rock, perhaps 50 meters deep. It stretched across the valley and heaped itself against the opposite mountain, cutting off the flow and promising to create what would soon be a lake. Jamie looked up where the cliff had been, to see a smooth gray scar suggesting the mountain's face had been scrubbed clean.

He sensed Amanda nearby.

"What about Alheeza? she asked.

"Oh shit! I forgot he should be coming back about now!"

"Can we reach him telepathically?" Amanda asked.

Jamie drew out his amulet, clutching the precious red stone in his left hand, he reached out with his mind: *Alheeza, were you caught in the rock slide? We were sheltered by the cave and are safe. Where are you? Are you all right? Can you hear me? Can you understand me?*

Jamie waited, but there was no response. He was about to put the stone back in his shirt when a faint message came through: *Hurt. Dark. Cannot move.*

*Did you pick any of that up?* Jamie mind-spoke.

*Yes, he is in great pain.*

"Oh shit!"

Slipping back into the darkened shelter, Jamie and Amanda quickly took inventory of their surviving gear. Amanda filled a pack with copeander, food and water, as well as what she thought might help for bandages.

Jamie pushed their pack, blankets and spears through the slot ahead of them as them climbed back out. After looking about, they prepared to ascend the rubble, that only minutes before had been the mountain side. The going was very difficult as they chambered from boulder to boulder.

While they puffed their way over the obstacles, Amanda said "He must be on the far side. If he had been close by, he would surely be dead!"

It was almost dark by the time they reached the far side of the rubble. Standing along the last of the big boulders, Jamie took out his crystal trying to reach Alheeza. With relief he sensed: *Hard to breath. Very thirsty. Come quickly.*

"He is close, I can sense it!" Jamie said with more confidence than he really felt. "I don't know if I can find him."

"Of course you can."

Jamie was standing with his crystal in his right hand as Amanda wrapped her arms around him. Drawing her own crystal out, she said, "Try again."

It took a few moments but they both heard in their heads, *I can feel you close. Come to me, I need you.*

Suddenly, Jamie had an image of Alheeza off to their right pinned between two boulders. "This way!" he shouted, feeling relieved to find their friend, but concerned about possible injuries.

Alheeza was trapped between two huge gray stones, his right hind leg crushed. The cut above his eye was crusted with dried blood.

Amanda poured her palms full of water for him to lap up while Jamie examined the pinning rock. He tried crouching to lift it, but nothing moved. Then Jamie tried using the blunt end of his spear shaft to lever it up, shifting the stone fractionally but not enough to free Alheeza.

"What if I try too?" Amanda asked.

"OK."

Using her smaller spear alongside of Jamie's, they managed to move the stone a hair. "Give it everything you've got!" strained Jamie.

He heard her grunt, and then there was a grinding noise as the rock shifted back and to the side several centimeters. Jamie mind-spoke: *Do you think you can crawl free?*

*I will try.*

Alheeza struggled, but his leg remained pinned in place. *You must try again, my friends.*

Together the pair adjusted their spear shafts and heaved up again. The rock lifted but did not slide away. Through gritting teeth Jamie said, "Try again!"

The humans heaved again, this time moving the boulder a few more centimeters. Through blinding pain Alheeza finally pulled his crushed leg free, just as Jamie slipped and the rock crashed back in place. Alheeza collapsed nearby.

Looking at his injuries, Amanda mind-spoke: *How bad is Alheeza and can we move you?*

*I think my leg is broken, but if you take care I expect I will be all right.*

Jamie scooped him up like a large baby, carrying him from the rubble to a flat space nearby while Amanda spread out one of their blankets for him to lie on. Then she crouched next to her injured friend studying him. As she struggled with how to assess his injuries, her hand unconsciously drew out her amber crystal. Suddenly, it seemed a veil was lifted for she knew the injured denzel had nothing more than what they'd already seen: a broken back leg, a deep cut to his head, and a number of bruises, but nothing life threatening. Dazed by the revelation, she looked down at her gem in wonder.

The smaller of Azimov-4's moons broke over the mountain top casting a dim yellow light over the disaster area. The light was poor, but it and her crystal allowed her to examine Alheeza's leg. Amanda could tell that Alheeza was in great pain, but he did not complain.

*The leg is broken just above his knee joint,* telepathed Amanda. *I'll need to set it. Can you find me a couple of flat sticks about this long?* She indicated with her hands.

*I will go look along the slide path.*

While he was gone, Amanda checked for other injuries on her friend. She found a good deal of swelling around his hip, but no more broken bones. Although the cut on his head looked bad, it had clotted over nicely.

*I think you got off lucky, my little friend. If you had been a meter in either direction we would have lost you.*

*Ah, you speak of luck. Is it good luck to be caught by falling rocks?*

*What I was really saying, is that I am very pleased that you did not get killed in the rock slide. I would have missed you very much.*

*Apparently, it was a time to hurt but not die.*

Amanda reached down to kiss the uninjured side of Alheeza's head.

Jamie's approach was not quiet, since he was dragging a good deal of shattered timber with him. Dropping his load, he poked around until he found the small pieces that he wanted. *Here, will these do?*

*I hope so.*

While she experimented with the sticks, he set about lighting a fire. By the flickering light of the flame, Amanda bound Alheeza's broken leg with two sticks wrapped securely with cord and then fed him a few slices of copeander and some more water. Soon he was asleep. After eating another cold meal of nuts, dried fruit and sliced tuber, the young couple settled down in front of the crackling fire.

Snuggling up to Jamie, Amanda was soon asleep. Dressed in only their jump-suits and woven vests, Jamie realized he would have to keep the fire going not only for protection from above but also for warmth, so he added what he hoped would be enough fuel. He put an arm around his special girl and drifted off. Unfortunately, it was not enough and he awoke shivering. Creeping forward he coaxed the flames back to life with fresh fuel. In the moonlight, he could see a lake forming behind the rock dam and realized that in the morning they would have to start moving before the water reached them. Amanda was sleeping next to Alheeza, so taking his spear in hand; he lay down behind them, wrapping his arm around Amanda. Eventually, he fell asleep again.

# They Came Quietly

The resilience of a denzel is a remarkable thing, or at least that is what the two humans believed. Alheeza had slept a good deal the first day, waking with a vigorous appetite. His nurse fussed over him until he almost purred.

*Our race has never cared for each other in the manner in which you do,* he mind-spoke to Amanda.

*Oh, I can leave you to fend for yourself if you want.*

He may not have been from their culture, but her smile betrayed any real threat of his care being withdrawn.

*I am feeling much better. I think I will try walking soon.*

*Really, you are ready for that after your injuries?*

Alheeza turned his head towards Jamie, who was curled under their carpet dome blanket, catching up on some much needed rest. Relocating them farther up the valley had taxed the last of his strength. For Jamie, picking his way back over the rock slide had been challenging, but he managed to bring a good deal of their undamaged supplies to the new campsite. Their old sleeping blanket along with a bag containing much of their food had been swept away, but everything else was recovered. The new campsite was not much more than a generous overhang with some large boulders standing between them and the river, but with a fire it had so far proved safe enough.

Amanda picked up a section of the carpet dome bark she had been working on and continued to punch small holes along the edge of the cut pattern. In the two days they had been nursing Alheeza, she had been able to finish most of their tunics. The rest of the foot coverings would be next.

Grunting next to her brought her attention back to Alheeza. He was struggling to stand.

*Here let me help you,* she mind-spoke.

*No. I can do this.*

He got up on three legs, but as he tried to put weight on his broken leg his stoic face revealed pain. After a moment he experimentally took a few steps, hopping only on his good back leg. *I am confident we can leave tomorrow. I am feeling an urgent call to the gathering.*

*If you are sure, then we leave tomorrow.*

"What is going on?" Jamie asked sleepily.

*Our injured partner says he is ready to continue the journey tomorrow.*

*Really?*

*Yes, the rain will have passed by then.*

*Rain?* Amanda mind-spoke.

*Yes, I smell rain coming.*

They'd already learned that when a denzel guide says it's going to rain, then it's best to prepare for the rain.

The cloud burst came not long after dark. The three travelers huddled at the back of their narrow shelter. In the first minutes the fire was extinguished and they were left to clutch each other for warmth. Jamie's usual excitement at touching Amanda was temporarily suspended as he held her close to his chest. Using his crystal to enhance his night vision, he peered out into the gloom searching for possible threats. Sleep finally overtook him.

He awoke in the predawn twilight to the sound of movement. Reflexively, he clutched his amulet, bringing his surroundings into sharp detail. Levering himself up on his elbow, Jamie stared out between the boulders. What he saw made his breath stop. A herd of tall creatures were soundlessly passing by. They must have stood as tall as him at the shoulder. Their slender silver bodies were ribbed along the torso. A particularly large one turned its head towards him as it passed. Its slim forked tongue flicked out to lick its snout, and then it shook its head making its long ears flop about, before continuing on.

*They are muzels, a herd animal that migrates through here this time of year,* Alheeza mind-spoke.

*Will the rock slide keep them from going further?*

*See for yourself.*

Stepping out from the boulders, Jamie looked back down the valley toward the rock slide. The herd hardly paused as it reached the boulder pile. Each one, including the young, jumped up, passing along the irregular course with an almost dancelike ease.

*It is time for me to join my kind.*

*Are you sure you are up to the task already?* telepathed Jamie.

With a nod, Alheeza took a few steps hopping on his good back leg. *Yes, it is time to be off.*

# Three Legs are Enough

It was more of a hop and twist than a steady gait. Amanda thought Alheeza must still be feeling a good deal of pain, since he carried his injured leg high. His breath came in gulps as he pushed his battered body forward.

They were making a steady pace up the narrow valley. By mid-morning, they came to the next rock slide. The quake had loosened more of the craggy slopes, and it was going to be difficult to make any speed across the rubble. The trio stopped at the edge of the slide where Alheeza gazed along the edge as if hoping to find an easier way.

*There is no other way but to cross the rock slide,* mind-spoke Jamie.

"How will Alheeza clamber over this kind of obstacle?"

Jamie slid his pack and attached supplies to the ground. Squatting, he mind-spoke: A*lheeza, I can carry you on my shoulders if you will allow it. It will conserve your strength for the easier trail beyond.*

*You cannot carry me and all of your belongings.*

*I'll make two trips, one with you and one for the rest of our equipment.*

Gazing beyond Jamie to the boulder pile that rose some distance above them, Alheeza responded: *You may carry me this time.*

Carefully, Amanda helped to position their denzel friend around Jamie's neck, supported by his shoulders. The injured leg stuck out over Jamie's left shoulder. While he reached up to hold his passenger by two of his good legs he asked in mind-speak: *Does this hurt?*

*It is tolerable. We may proceed.*

Jamie took a few experimental steps up into the rubble heap and stopped. "Amanda, please pass me my long spear. I will use it as a staff while I climb."

Holding Alheeza's foreleg and his good back leg with one hand, Jamie set off again, leaping from stone to stone with his staff to steady him. It was an arduous journey for both, but Alheeza never complained as Jamie readjusted his burden to try to keep him as comfortable as possible. In twenty minutes they had traversed the slide area. As Jamie gently set Alheeza down, his friend telepathed: *I am grateful for your assistance.*

*My pleasure.*

———————◇———————

It was mid-afternoon, and as the trail became wider, all three soon walked or limped abreast.

*The tremor that caused these slides has changed so much of the landscape that I can no longer trust my ancestral memories. It has become difficult for me to see what lies ahead.*

*Are you worried about selecting a campsite for tonight?* mind-spoke Amanda.

*Yes.*

*Then we shall just have to keep an eye out for a place that gives us some protection.*

The river was stronger here, churning over and around embedded boulders, the sound of the crashing waves echoed within the valley. Jamie's breath was starting to labour with the steady climb. As they made their way up the trail, vegetation had dwindled, and the air was taking on a chill. Amanda's needle work had given him a generous tunic that came most of the way to his knees and elbows. Without these new garments it would be really cold later. Also he started to worry about making a fire for the evening. Where was he going to get the fuel?

*There used to be a plateau not far ahead,* mind-spoke Alheeza.

*Good,* replied Amanda.

As they plodded along, there was little conversation; each was lost in their own thoughts.

The steep walls of the valley took a sharp turn, and there before them was a slot of blue sky with wisps of high cloud. What made Jamie smile was the purple green of vegetation ahead. It did not look like the dry forest they had spent so much time in, but it was lush just the same.

In half an hour, they were standing on the edge of a narrow valley. The mountains on the other side seemed even higher, capped with glistening snow. Even here, the evidence of rockslides could be seen. New scars were visible on a few of the mountain faces. Before them, the valley had a dense growth of low bushes or trees that appeared to block their way.

Alheeza was still puffing noticeably while he mind-spoke: *The valley seems relatively unchanged. You cannot see it, but there is a well-defined trail ahead that leads to the lake. There may even be some delicacies along the lake.*

*Food is good!* exclaimed Amanda in mind-speak.

*It does look promising!* added Jamie.

There was a trail through the tightly woven tangle of growth. Whatever animal used this trail was shorter than Jamie, for he had to stoop to keep from being lashed in the face. Before long, they were standing near the shore of a rippling lake. A low hedge of vegetation with thick stocks and bulbous tops, formed a barricade.

*We call these cat-balls. If we dig, you may find the roots will make a tasty addition to our food stock,* mind-spoke Alheeza.

Using her spear as a digging tool, Amanda soon was turning up yellow bulbs from around the roots. Jamie took an interest in the orb-like tops. Some were red and fleshy, while the mature ones had turned a leathery brown. When he slit the side of one, it burst open with a fluffy white center. Jamie smiled as he pulled out his magnifying glass. Shining a hot spot of light on it, soon brought a trickle of smoke. It burst into flame like a flare. "Holly shit!' he exclaimed as he stepped back from the heat.

"What mischief are you up to?" asked Amanda.

"Oh, just experimenting with the local flora!"

"Well, don't burn down the place before we can have supper."

"I don't think it will spread. Look, the fire stays contained around the top capsule of the cat-balls, and the growth around the bottom is damp. I think it will be fine if I just leave it to burn out."

*I did not know the old tops burned, but we have no history of fire as you know. The bulbs are another matter, and I hope you enjoy them as much as my race has,* telepathed Alheeza.

*Where should we make camp?* asked Jamie in mind-speak.

*You have solved the problem of this evening's fire, so I will show you the kind of bush that our race often shelter under.*

---

Not far back from the lake, the land rose high enough so that the ground was no longer spongy and wet. The bushes that Alheeza chose were like large fans that stretched out over a small meadow. Amanda crouched under the overlapping fronds of the branches that formed a sort of roof. She experimentally felt the woolly ground cover, and found it very soft to touch.

*I think we are going to have our first comfortable bed in many days, my friends.*

Alheeza flopped down in the lush growth, sighing with relief. *That does feel nice. I do not think I could have traveled any farther today.*

Amanda telepathed: *I am still amazed at your endurance, especially so soon after you were hurt.*

*Rest will help, and maybe a sliver of the copeander as well,* mind-spoke Alheeza as he lay his head in the soft grey ground cover.

Jamie dropped his large arm load of cat-ball tops. He stomped around in front of the bush shelter, trying to decide how to best make the evening fire. At length, he deciding to sprinkle some of their water around his chosen spot, and then light one of the bulbs. As it burst into flame the ground cover wilted around it. Some of it nearest to the fire smoldered and went out. Sitting back, Jamie said to himself, "Well that went better than I hoped."

*Sometimes you are just lucky!* added Amanda.

---

The meal of roasted cat-ball roots was spectacular, maybe the best tasting vegetable to date. Alheeza had fallen asleep as soon as he had eaten his raw tubers, while the humans had chosen to roast the last of theirs. The raw ones were good, but the roasting brought out a flavour that was remarkable. Now they lounged, spooned together on the soft ground cover before the small fire, the cat-ball fluff having been replaced with dry branches collected from around the meadow. Amanda's new tunic helped make the evening chill tolerable.

Except for the star field above, the clearing was dark when Jamie awoke, unsure what had awakened him. He reached into his tunic and drew out the ruby stone. It glowed a dull red in the dark. When he clasped it firmly, he knew in an instant why he was awake. A Great Raptor was approaching, and as he looked off to the side, he could see a shadow coming across the stars. Cold fear raced through his body. There was no hiding here in the low bushes. They were alone and exposed.

With only seconds to react, Jamie jumped up groping for his knife. Letting his crystal dangle, he opened the large blade on his metal knife. Grabbing the first cat-ball within reach he split it open, shaking segments of the white fluff onto their ashes. On hands and knees, he blew gently while prodding the coals. There was a flicker of red as an ember glowed. In the next instant, a flame burst from the fragments of fluff. Quickly he cut open three more balls just as he felt, more than heard, the deep throb of descending wings. The cat-balls flared and he held the flaming brand high above him. There was shouting and screaming as the red-eyed nemesis beat the air just short of the meadow. Holding the bright torch in his left hand, he raised the crystal amulet in the other. Only then did he hear himself shouting, "Back, you demon. Get back, I warn you!"

Amanda awoke when Jamie pulled his arm out from under her head. Now he was screaming at the top of his lungs, holding a flaming branch in the air. She could not breathe as she watched, paralyzed as the drama between the Great Raptor and the young man played out in front of her.

Later she would remember in remarkable detail: the feeling of the air pounding as the Raptor beat its great wings to avert its dive,

Jamie standing with the cluster of cat-balls blazing white in one hand, his voice repeating the challenge as he thrust his glowing red crystal into the air, and how utterly quiet it was after the creature had departed.

Someone was crying…

---

*Alheeza watched the humans as the male held his distraught mate in his arms. These were truly amazing beings, apparently irrational in one instance, and incredibly resourceful in others. He knew in his core that his survival in these past moon cycles had been linked to the one called Jamie. Had there been no human fire, he, too, would have gone the way of his genetic elders.*

*The gathering was close now and they would leave at first light.*

# In Between Mountains

J amie shook his head as he tried to add up the days since he and his father had crashed into the glade. Each night he'd scratched a line on the side of a drinking container. There were now 61 marks, that was about two months and yet it felt like years.

They'd laboured up the valley for the past two days, through some very rugged terrain, all changed since the earth quake. It was late morning, and now they stood looking down on a wide area with three converging valleys. It was not lush, nor was it barren. Jamie noticed shrubs surrounding a small lake in the valley's center and along the tributaries leading to it.

Alheeza had been surprisingly mute today, apparently lost in his own thoughts. His leg seemed to be healing but he still hopped along on three legs. He broke the silence: *This is the valley of the great denzel gathering. I must go down ahead of you. If the introductions go well, I will beckon you.*

Without further conversation, he made his way down the narrow trail.

Her mother had called them butterflies. Amanda had never seen a real butterfly, but she guessed the fluttering feeling of anxiety she was experiencing, must be something like a stomach filled with them. To steel herself for yet another unknown encounter she sat down with her gear spread out. Drawing out the delicate needle and fibrous thread, along with scraps of carpet dome, she said, "Jamie come and lend me your foot for a minute."

Jamie, who had been preoccupied with his own feelings of trepidation, turned to look at her. "What are you planning now?"

"Alheeza says that the final pass beyond here may take us through even colder conditions. I thought some foot wear would be good. Remember the moccasin patterns from the Wilderness Survival book? I thought I would work on a pair for both of us while we wait for our guide to return."

"That seems fair," said Jamie as he sat before her, extending a somewhat grubby callused foot.

It was now mid-afternoon and Jamie was starting to worry about what was happening with Alheeza. At first he had helped punch some holes in the moccasin cut-outs, and after that he pulled out his flinger.

"What are you making now?" Amanda asked.

"Oh, I thought it was time to work out some of the glitches in this projectile device."

As she watched, he placed a smooth blunt stick in the slot while drawing the red elastic back over it. It fit over a wooden pin, and as Jamie pointed his device along the path he released the crude trigger. The arrow shot out at a blinding speed, only to curve off to the side as it slewed sideways. Jamie's face was one of complete disappointment. Slowly he rose from his cross-legged position, and went to retrieve his arrow. Returning he muttered, "If I just had some sort of little wing on the back, the book suggests using feathers, but there is nothing like that on this planet."

Amanda looked down at the trimmings from her work on their moccasins. "What if I tied a little flap of this onto the back of it?"

"What?" Jamie looked startled.

Amanda held up a small triangle of shoe trimming. "Here, give it to me for a moment."

He watched with fascination as she deftly re-trimmed the section and bound it to the back of his shaft with a fine cord. "Here, try it again."

This time the slender shaft flew with blurred speed without swerving to the side. Jamie whooped as he jumped in the air. "You're amazing! Did you see that, it went right where I was pointing it!"

"It looked pretty good to me!"

Jamie was about to reach over to her when he realized there were tears in her eyes. "What's wrong?"

"I'm on edge waiting to see what happens with Alheeza and his kind."

"Yeah, I'm a bit on edge too."

"I had better finish my chores."

Jamie tried to focus on placing a tiny glass shard on an arrow point, but his heart was not in it. He sat brooding, looking down into the valley hoping to catch a glimpse of Alheeza returning.

Amanda's hand rested on his shoulder, "Try this on."

When he turned to look up at her, his eye settled on a brown rough boot that she held out to him. "I don't think it matters which foot you put it on. The fit will be imprecise. I thought it might be more comfortable with the soft stuff on the inside."

While he pulled a boot onto his right foot, he felt the soft fur-like fiber caress his foot. It was a bit loose, but as he stood, he could feel the warmth and protection that the tough material gave to his step. "Oh, this feels wonderful!" he said, as he spun about on the new moccasin.

"You look like a little kid at solstice gift-giving time!" exclaimed Amanda.

In a flash he took her under the armpits, hoisting her above his head. "And you are the best gift ever!"

As he slowly brought her down, she wrapped her arms around his neck. The embrace brought their bodies in full contact. They shivered almost simultaneously as their lips met. It was a long, lingering kiss. Amanda was the first to open her mouth, sweeping her tongue around the perimeter of his lips. Excitement surged through his body, and he held her tight.

How long had they been locked in their caressing embrace, they didn't know? It was Alheeza's mind-spoken message that interrupted the lustful moment.

*The elders are prepared to meet you. Come with me.*

Amanda slid to the ground as Jamie slowly released her. They both were flushed and breathing heavily as they looked down at their denzel friend.

*It would be best if you could accompany me as quickly as possible. I do not want to give the elders a reason to change their minds. Bring all of your gear with you.*

# In Hot Water

J amie was daydreaming about the passage of time. Ever since the loss of all their technology, time had become an estimate. So far their hike felt it took 45-minutes. They were following Alheeza over rough ground with outcrops of blue-green spiked vegetation. Their packs with assorted bags and pouches flopped and banged, making Jamie painfully aware of how different they would look to a community of denzels.

They stopped at the entrance to a blind canyon, with steep walls and deep shadows. Two large denzels stepped out as if to block their advance.

Cautioned by Alheeza, both humans remained silent in either form of speech. There was obviously some sort of silent dialog between their guide and the sentries. The larger of the two apparent guards, looked up at them, and his expression was malevolent. Amanda's hand sought Jamie's while they awaited the next move.

Finally, Alheeza, turned back to them. *Follow behind me in single file. Do not communicate in any way until I give the signal.*

Jamie sensed that his companion had selectively communicated with them, just like the meeting with the sentries. He had not realized that mind-speak could be directed. The trio ahead moved on, and they followed.

Behind Jamie, Amanda was taking in the changing surroundings. What had looked like a bleak canyon was, revealed to be one with numerous craters scattered throughout the narrow valley. Within each depression, was a lush growth of vegetation that she had not seen before. Clusters of thick fleshy leaves sprouted from a central core, to a height of about two meters. Many of these dark green-gray shafts had a large swollen protrusion about half way up. Some had been broken off near the base. Before she could speculate any further about the nature of these plants, the group came to a stop.

She could see sweat beading on Jamie's cheek, and she knew he was also suffering anxiety about this meeting of the races. As if on some silent command, denzels started to step out from boulders. In just a few moments, there must have been hundreds of the pale green eyes upon them.

Amanda watched as Alheeza lowered his chest to the ground, in a form of obedience, before the gathering. She tugged on Jamie's tunic before going to her knees and bending forward, hoping to imitate Alheeza's gesture as best a human could. Jamie's elbow brushed hers as he lowered himself beside her.

Time seemed to drag and then Alheeza's familiar voice caressed her mind within: *Come and stand beside me, both of you.*

Amanda found herself looking into the intelligent eyes of what appeared to be five old denzels. How she knew they were elders of the community, she wasn't sure. Maybe it was their penetrating stare, or perhaps the way they stood compared to their young guide, but she knew these were important members of Alheeza's world.

As they stepped beside him, Alheeza continued in their telepathic form of speech: *I present before you the aliens from the stars. I know them as Jamie Chambers and Amanda Martin. I testify on my ancestor's memories that these creatures have done me great service since my genetic elders were taken by the Great Ones.*

A new pattern of mind-speak was heard in their heads: *Alheeza the younger, you have testified before the elders of this gathering that these alien creatures have traveled upon the same journey as you. Many of the strange things you have declared make little sense, and we withhold judgment until they have been examined completely. Before we start, they must be cleansed, for their alien smell offends our olfactory senses. Let it be done.*

Alheeza dipped his head twice, and without looking at the humans he telepathed: *Follow me.*

In single file again, Jamie and Amanda trailed behind Alheeza as he worked his way towards the back of the blind canyon. Curious denzels stepped aside to the let the trio pass. No further communication was detected as they passed. Before long, they were climbing a smooth slope with contoured ridges stacked upon each other.

As they ascended the slope, Amanda whispered, "Do we smell that bad, Alheeza?"

*I have grown accustomed to your presence. Also, I know that since leaving Sanctuary, your usual bathing practice has been suspended.*

It appeared to be a well-worn path that the three of them followed. It took them well away from the populated part of the valley. Soon they were climbing a steep narrow track that led to a plateau. Jamie picked up a hint of sulphur before the hot pools were visible. As they stepped over the ledge, the water spread out before them.

*There are three descending pools here. The topmost is smallest but also the hottest. Each pool mixes with cold water until you have this one before you.*

Amanda bent to place a hand in the pool. Unlike the stream she had bathed in back at Sanctuary, this was warm. She had not bathed in warm water since she was aboard Mayflower.

*The elders have decreed that you must be cleansed before your examination, this cannot be changed. There are about three of your earth hours until the sun sets. I will come back before half of that time has passed.*

*Alheeza, I know we are expected to bathe, but if we put our travel clothing back on, will we not still smell?* mind-spoke Amanda.

*In the early part of our journey, I observed that you dipped clothing in water to remove the grime. Can you not do the same here?*

*The material will still be wet and, as you have observed, we feel chilled in damp clothing,* Amanda telepathed.

*Use your uncanny resourcefulness, or do not put them back on.*

Jamie and Amanda looked at each other as Alheeza turned to leave.

Amanda sensed Jamie's awkwardness and took the lead by setting their gear aside. She pulled out their soiled clothing, saying, "It seems that we must bath to keep from offending their noses.

177

To be truthful, we have been hiking over this rough country and all personal cleanliness from the days on the Mayflower has gone by the wayside. Let's take these garments up to the hottest pool and scrub them first. We should be able to dry the thin jumpsuits a good deal if we wring them out well afterwards."

Jamie followed quietly as they climbed to the topmost pool. The surface was smooth and wet, making it slippery in places. Soon they stood looking down into the uppermost pool several meters across. Wisps of steam rose from the hot surface and Amanda's nose wrinkled at the sulphurous odor.

Jamie kneeled beside her, dipping one of his jumpsuits in the hot pool. His fingers stung at first, but as he swished his garment around, it started to feel very nice. Looking over, Amanda was scrubbing hers briskly over the ribs of the pool edge. Dunking it one more time she brought it out and wrung the water from it. Holding it to her nose, she said, "I have to say this hot water took the dirt out a lot faster than the cold stream back at our cave."

Once Jamie's old jump-suit was washed and wrung out, they placed both suits on a warm, dry ledge.

"I know that you are hesitant to bathe with me for fear of being aroused, but I think the hot water will temper that," said Amanda, pulling the crude carpet-dome garment over her head. She turned her back on Jamie as she drew the seal of her oversized jump-suit open, letting it drop to the ground. Pulling off the delicate undershirt and briefs, she stepped towards the steaming pool.

Jamie held his breath as he watched the beautiful curves on Amanda's body descend into the hot pool. His hands shook as he pulled his own crude tunic over his head. He had wanted this moment to happen, and now he was afraid of it as well. As his undershorts fell around his ankles, he cautiously turned back towards the pool. Amanda was immersed up to her neck, respectfully facing away from him. The water stung his feet as he edged into the pool. Just as Amanda had said, his arousal faded as the hot water engulfed his genitals. He let out his breath as he edged farther into stinging water.

Amanda turned to face him, her green eyes flashing. She studied the muscular young man easing towards her. His thick dark hair with its slight wave now hung almost to his shoulders. Gleaming upon his light chest hair was the red crystal, suspended by the fine cord that she had prepared. As their eyes met she said, "You look like a fine human specimen, an excellent example of our species to put forward to the race of denzels."

Breathlessly, Jamie replied, "You're gorgeous!"

Standing navel deep in the pool he gazed at her piercing emerald eyes. Amanda rose from her squatting position, stepping towards him. Her torso slipped from the water, Jamie took in the marvel before him: the narrow shoulders, slim but muscular arms, firm rounded breasts with dark nipples, and a light flashed from her amber crystal. She was a goddess incarnate.

Jamie tried to say something clever but just stood there agape. She came towards him, wrapping her arms around his neck. Amanda whispered something about him being her soul mate, but it was the touch of her lips, and the thrill of her naked body pressed against him that he would remember forever.

# Fire From Nothing

Alheeza pushed his exhausted body up the glistening slope towards the hot pools. He could hear the human laughter that he had come to understand as something good in his strange friends. They were pulling on their light jumpsuits, over what appeared to be naked bodies. Something had changed since he had left them here.

*You must be examined by the elder before full darkness, so hurry my friends:* mind-spoke Alheeza.

*We are as ready as we will ever be*: smiled Amanda.

Jamie kneeled to gather their gear together. Along with their handmade garments, small items from the ship, food, water, and weapons, he also had a cluster of the dried orbs on stems from the marsh. Swinging his own pack over his shoulder, Jamie helped Amanda into her cumbersome pack. Each gathered the rest of their collection into their hands and stood ready to leave.

*Since your elders wanted us clean, I thought we would just wear these rinsed out jumpsuits and later we can put on the warmer clothing. There was no time to clean and dry all of it,* mind-spoke Amanda.

*That seems fair; follow me,* telepathed Alheeza as he set off with his three-legged gait.

The path back was now devoid of all onlookers.

"Where have they all gone?" asked Amanda.

*Night approaches, most have retired to the family corners. We will be meeting the wisest of my race in the gathering cave.*

Deep within the valley, everything was cast in shadow. The sky above had a hint of gold foretelling of sunset not far away. Jamie could see subtle details that were hidden in the strong shadows of the afternoon. From the edges of some of the caverns, he could see individual denzels staring out at him.

*How long has your race been coming here, Alheeza?* mind-spoke Jamie.

*Beyond memory. Stay quiet as we approach the gathering cave.*

The blind canyon had three separate short arms. Each one ended in a steep rock face, but the one they had just turned towards had a gaping wide opening that spanned most of the narrow valley floor. As they made their way over the rocky surface, details of the approaching cave became clearer.

There were no sentries here, just a well-worn path that led straight into the wide mouth of the cavern. As the path rose up through boulders, it opened into a smooth open area with an enormous vaulted ceiling above.

Amanda stood spellbound, staring at the ceiling. "There are dots of light flying about," she whispered.

*Quiet and follow me, they are waiting!* insisted Alheeza.

It was not long before they stood before the five elder denzels, who stared at them without expression.

Alheeza made his deferential gesture to the elders, and they each, in turn, did their best to imitate him.

*Alheeza the Younger, you have told us that the alien intruders have some crude way of communicating with you. How is this so?*

Alheeza turned to Jamie, nodding: *This is where you express yourself.*

Taking a deep breath, Jamie slid the seam of his suit open to reveal his precious red stone. In slow movements, he grasped his crystal, looking into the eyes of the elder denzel standing slightly ahead of the rest. He mind-spoke: *I am Jamblyn Chambers, from beyond the stars. My friends, including Alheeza, call me Jamie. Without Alheeza's expert knowledge of this land, we would have perished.* Gesturing towards Amanda he continued, *This is my mate, Amanda Martin. We, along with our families traveled the length of my lifetime, across the stars, to find a new home. We come with no intention of harming your race, and seek only to live in harmony.*

In unison, the elders staggered, as if being hit by a shock wave.

After a pause, the denzel replied, *How can this be?*

Jamie turned to look at his companions trying to grasp what he needed to do next. Finally, he plunged on: *In the beginning, when there was just my father and me, I started to get feelings or ideas that seemed to come from nowhere. It turned out that I was picking up very simple thoughts from Alheeza. Not mind-speak, just a vague feeling about things like hunger and thirst. That is how I found my first food and water. After the Great Raptors killed Alheeza's family, we seemed to be traveling in the same direction. After my father was killed, (Jamie held his amulet a little higher) suddenly I could hear Alheeza's thoughts in my head. Now we are here and you can understand me. I have no better explanation, but I am grateful that we can understand each other.*

Amanda blinked back tears, for she had never heard Jamie speak so succinctly. Oh, how she loved this man!

Alheeza intervened: *I have tried to explain, these beings are intelligent, resourceful, and compassionate. What you have to see is how they can use their hands to change things. I have made testimony that without their assistance I, too, would have perished. As to how they can speak in our thought language, I can only say that the crystals seem to have aided their ability to communicate.*

In the moments that followed, the old denzels drew close together, conferring in their quiet way. The most senior member turned towards the newcomers again: *Your apparent intelligence is surprising, but that you can speak in our manner of speech is beyond belief. That you also claim that you have traveled here across the stars is unimaginable. We can only trust the observations of Alheeza the Younger, and your own testimony, which appears to have truth. We must speak more on these matters, but first introductions must be made.*

Jamie's head spun as each of the elders made formal introductions. He remembered the first one best, *Alazar,* their senior elder, along with his mate Muhara. He was aware of the other names, but their strangeness made them hard to remember, he would ask Alheeza to coach him on the names later.

After the formal introductions were done, they were shown to the back of the cave where a stream of hot water gurgled from a slot in the rock wall. It flowed into a shallow steaming pool before continuing along its way along the valley floor. The three travelers settled on the warm ground to continue their discussions with the elders. Several smaller denzels approached, carrying something in their mouths. In a deferential way, a plump node was dropped beside each of the members. Amanda noted that it was the same plants she had seen near the entrance.

*You are now being treated as guests, these are offerings of food. It is customary to consume these before the conversations continue.*

Amanda picked up the elliptical offering, bringing it to her nose. It had a pungent smell that was not altogether pleasing. Looking up, she could see Jamie examining his food as well. The denzels were munching contentedly on theirs, so she took an experimental bite. She had to admit it tasted a good deal better than it smelled, but its pasty texture seemed to stick to her pallet. She picked up one of their water jugs to wash the last of it down. The simple act of taking a drink seemed to have frozen their hosts in place.

It was Alheeza that broke the silence: *This is just one example of how they manipulate their environment. As you can see they can carry water with them, making it possible to travel farther in the dry lands. True, they get thirsty much sooner than we do, but still, it offers a great compensation for their diminished capacities.*

After their simple meal, the questions started. Where exactly did Alheeza find them? How did their bond grow? There was a great deal of interest around the failed Raptor attacks. It was agreed that the greater questions of Jamie and Amanda's extraordinary trip across the galaxy would have to wait.

*It is time to show them fire from nothing,* mind-spoke Alheeza.

Jamie knew this was going to be a critical time and he had carefully prepared his supplies for this moment. His old Swiss Army knife was looking shabby from the weeks of constant use as both a knife and fire striker. Placing his driest tinder before him, he positioned the fire stone adjacent to it. Without looking up, Jamie drew in a deep breath, and then in one smooth motion, he brought down the back of the knife on the hard rock. Several sparks tumbled into the tinder. No smoke rose, so he hit the rock another blow. A few more sparks cascaded about the tinder. This time a curl of smoke rose from the edge. Quickly, he bent to blow on the spot. Caressing the little plume with his breath, a glow appeared, followed by a small flame. Quickly he added more dry tinder fluff, followed by small cracked twigs. The flame grew quickly.

Amanda had been holding her breath, but as Jamie's face was illuminated by the growing flame, she felt herself relax. It was foolish to worry about the first fire for the elders, but still so much hinged on making a good impression. She glanced over to their hosts; they had drawn back, eyes round with amazement.

Again it was Alheeza who broke the silence: *As you can see, the human can draw fire where none had been before. I have seen him do this repeatedly. It was how he kept the Great Raptors, not to mention other predators, at bay.*

# They Came From the Sky

---

J amie had taken the role of primary spokesperson, and Amanda was content to let him explain as much as he could. Looking up at the high ceiling, she again watched in fascination at the swarms of little bright lights that darted about. The glow from their activity made it possible to see most things about the cave. In a pause in the discussion, she mind-spoke: *Elders, please tell me about the luminescent dots that I see dancing above us?*

Muhara looked over to her, mind-speaking: *Within this cave, the glow-flyers make their nests. By giving the nest a little nudge, it rouses them to fly about our gathering.*

*Thank you, elder, I find them fascinating.*

*You are a curious creature, Amanda from beyond the stars. Come with me, I think it is time we carried on our own conversations while I show you some of these nests.*

Walking back towards the entrance, Amanda found it easy to communicate with Muhara. The ease that she had built from weeks with Alheeza seemed to transfer easily to the gracious elder. It was still mind-speak, but somehow it had a feminine touch, more feeling and less aloof.

The nests themselves looked somewhat spiny, but upon closer inspection, it was a small orb covered with a multitude of the rigid, winged little creatures protruding outward. What she assumed were their snouts faced away from the center, the little folded wings were yellow framed with black, and somehow they were attached to the orb by the end of their abdomen. As Muhara nudged the edge of it, a cluster of the little winged creatures took to the air. Each one's body began to glow the moment it started to fly.

Amanda could not help smiling as she was surrounded by the twinkly lights: *They are so beautiful!* She mind-spoke. *How long does each of them live?*

*What a strange question, but they live a long time compared to other small flying creatures.*

*What do they feed on?*

*That ball they rest upon is a dropping from a swamp-bellower. It lasts for more than a set of season cycles.*

*Would it hurt them to be contained in a much smaller place?*

*I have no way of knowing, but it is possible.*

Amanda slid her small carrying bag from her shoulder. Opening it she rummaged around until she drew out one of the clear storage bags.

*May I try something? I will try not to hurt any of the glow-flyers, but I want to contain them for a short while.*

Carefully she opened the bag, holding it wide with her fingers, she dropped it over one of the nests. Using her fingers carefully she lifted the glow-flyers perch until she could draw the seal of the bag closed underneath it. As soon as she had picked it up the rest of the residents had taken off within the enclosure. A warm light washed over the pair of them as Amanda held the bag aloft.

*How did you know to do that?* asked Muhara.

*I do not know how to explain, but we have had need of a portable light in our travels, and I thought this might offer some way of doing it.*

*You really are a curious race, but I see no harm as long you set them free at a later time.*

*As you wish.*

---

It was growing late, and the exertions of the day left Jamie exhausted. He tried to focus on the subject at hand while he absentmindedly fingered his stone: *Elders, our people have learned over hundreds of years, how to make a vessel that would travel unimaginable distances across the stars. I do not know how to make a starship, but there were those among us that did. As Alheeza told you already, something happened when the sun suddenly became over bright, and our traveling machines were destroyed. We lack the ability to make new ships again, leaving the survivors here marooned. There is no way of getting back to our home world now. The two of us have learned a great deal from Alheeza about making a living from the land. We only wish to live in harmony with you, and the other races that inhabit your planet.*

Alazar mind-spoke: *We have no ancestral memories that help to guide us in this matter. What you have been telling us is so far beyond anything we could imagine, that it will take a good deal of discussion and contemplation on our part before we can assimilate your story. There seems to be no falseness in your being, and that will be taken into consideration.*

Amanda and Muhara rejoined the group, each one settling beside their kind. In the pause that followed their arrival, Amanda drew out her clear inflated bag mind-speaking: *Elders, Muhara has given her permission to share this.* She shook the transparent container, making it burst forth with a steady glow.

*What kind of magic is this?* asked Alazar turning towards Muhara.

*The female human has made a portable environment for the glow-flyers. I sense no real disruption in their lives other than reducing their flight area,* responded Muhara.

Jamie reached over to touch the glow bag: *You have made portable light without a fire. Wonderful!*

An animated discussion followed the arrival of the container of glow-flyers. Jamie sat beaming with pride at Amanda's innovation, when suddenly he felt a chill. Clasping his ruby stone the feeling became more intense. Somewhere in his unconscious, he knew what was about to happen. Full night had come, bringing with it the terror from above.

*Elders, Great Raptors approach!* he mind-spoke.

*This cannot be. Our sentries have not given the alert!* telepathed Alazar.

There was a strained silence as the two species stared at each other. Jamie was about to repeat his concerns when shrieks broke

187

out from the valley below. This was mixed with the unmistakable sound of large Raptor wings beating the air in descent, followed almost immediately by their attack scream. The night's terror had arrived.

Claws scraped on stone at the mouth of their cave. A terrifying bellow reverberated within the cavern, followed by the foul stench of the Raptor's breath. In the dim light of the agitated glow-flyers, Jamie could make out the shape of the largest Raptor he had ever seen. The massive cave which had seemed so inviting in the afternoon now felt like a death trap.

Quickly glancing back, Jamie saw Amanda's terrified eyes, but what stunned him was the almost frozen look upon the elder's lean faces. He telepathed: *What do you do when they attack?*

*It has never happened like this before. We are already at the deepest part of the cave and there is no escape!* came Alazar's response.

Instinctively, Jamie dropped to the ashes of his little fire. He smashed open a dry cat-ball, extracting some of its dry fiber from within. His hands shook as he willed himself to focus on the task at hand. Trying to ignore the approaching Raptor; he blew on a single smoldering coal, coaxed a delicate flame from within. He sensed the approaching Raptor, and it made his guts twist with fear, fumbling with a cat-ball he dropped it into his tiny flame. A fresh wave of stench swept over him as the great predator crept ever closer. The next scream was so close he could feel the heat from its putrid breath. As the makeshift torch caught fire, Jamie held it aloft.

As it flared, it illuminated the glistening scales on the raptor's massive head, its red eyes burning in fury while its gaping mouth revealed jagged yellow teeth. As Jamie thrust the fire higher, the creature twisted its head to the side, exposing its colossal size, for this raptor's dorsal fin stood taller than Jamie. The length of its neck and wing span was beyond his reckoning. A jolt of fear like he'd never felt before made him freeze.

Behind him, Amanda shrieked, apparently, more in anger than fear, thus breaking the spell. Jamie again thrust his flaming torch towards the massive predator. It bellowed in response, and the force of its stench almost knocked him back. This time, he thrust the flame at his attacker's snout. It recoiled, allowing Amanda time to step forward to light their last two cat-balls from the flame of his torch.

As the torch flared up, the Great Raptor jerked back again, turning its head from side to side as if the brightness was too hard to look at. Sensing some advantage, Jamie thrust his torch forward again, while holding his brilliant ruby crystal high in the air. As it gleamed red from a light within, he heard his own voice screaming loudly, **"Get away from her you vile creature. You have no place here. LEAVE US NOW!"**

Despite his appearance of bravado, Jamie knew their supply of cat-balls was depleted. If they failed, disaster would follow. Sensing Jamie's sudden doubt, Amanda started waving her two flaming cat-balls about, leaving trails of sparks in the air. At this new threat, the creature slowly began a retreat. Emboldened, Jamie mimicked Amanda's approach and the two of them backed the Great Raptor to the edge of the cavern. Without hesitation, it turned and took off into the night sky. Soon, the air was filled with other departing Raptors, their broad wings beating the air, as they climbed out of the valley. But unlike their arrival, their departure was accompanied by the wailing of captured or injured denzels.

Feeling Amanda at his side, Jamie slipped an arm over her shoulder. She put hers around his waist, saying in a hoarse voice, "What a team we make!"

# Alliance

W as he awake? Jamie couldn't be sure. Images of the slavering Raptor bellowing its attack clung to the periphery of his vision. In the distorted manner of dreaming, he couldn't make a fire, and it seemed so close to catching him this time. Slowly, muted details of the cave roof became visible. In his mind he knew it was just another dream, but he felt as drained as if it had really happened.

Curled next to the dying embers of their small fire, he was clothed in his carpet-dome garments; he was warm enough, especially since he was holding the still sleeping Amanda to his chest. The memories of the past week came back to him in an involuntary flood of screams, huge dark flying creatures, the urgency to care for the injured and finally the nights of tending the protective ring of fires. He was awake but exhausted.

Amanda stirred in his arms, triggering his other memories. Naked bodies pressed close together, the exploration of new frontiers and the unexpected release of his pent up urgency. They were inexperienced lovers but she was so patient with him. How could such terrible events take place so close to such a wonderful loving experience?

As Amanda's breath slipped back into the rhythm of sleep, Jamie relaxed remembering the days before, and how all barriers between the denzels and them had evaporated after the Raptor attack. He had a new respect for these quiet creatures, in the way they comforted their injured companions, and the silent ceremony releasing their dead.

The denzels considered Jamie and Amanda as heroes—curious creatures—but heroes nevertheless. They asked Jamie and

Amanda to stoke fires in front of the big caves as a preventative measure against possible attack; it was the first of the interspecies cooperation. With instructions, denzels sought out deadfall, dragging individual pieces back so that at dusk, Jamie and Amanda would start the six protective fires. During the night, they took turns sleeping and stoking the fires.

Sliding his arm free from Amanda, Jamie rose to meet the morning, "Will I ever feel rested again?" he muttered to himself as he stepped out into the brightening canyon.

---

The couple were hoping to leave soon to seek out Base Camp, so Amanda had her own set of chores to tend to today. Jamie was still with the elders, sharing the last details before their planned departure. The sun had just gone behind the cliff and she was taking the rest of their clean clothing up to the private cave that had been granted by the elders. These long living creatures were fascinating, especially the few very young ones. Four of them followed her now, like a shadow, eager to see what other marvels she might produce. Just the act of scrubbing the dirt out of their travel clothes seemed to cause great delight. When she pulled out Jamie's knife and started to trim the last bits of dome-carpet, they danced about in apparent joy. She smiled at how much pleasure these youngsters had given her. When she reached the lip of their cave, her entourage stopped, apparently they were forbidden to enter this area. Squatting to look them in the eye, she mind-spoke: *Little ones, we leave soon, but I will see you again tomorrow morning.*

They danced off down the slope, stopping to look back from time to time. Amanda turned back to her chores and it was not long afterwards that she heard Jamie approaching. He was carrying a bundle of dried stocks, and he tossed them down at the side of their gear before reaching over to embrace her.

Before long, several of the local bulbs roasted in the coals at the edge of a small fire. Amanda leaned against Jamie's chest saying, "Have you asked them about Base Camp?"

"That is tomorrow's subject, today it was more about our family lineage, our general history, and how the written word works."

"You did not get into the computers, and how they saved so much more?"

"I tried to keep it simple; after all, I had the old book and tried to show him how it worked. Even that proved to be a challenge. In their culture it is all about memories, and as Alheeza tried to tell us, there is some sort of link with present and past memories. Now, that is hard for me to grasp. I guess that is our real difference."

"So different, and yet watching the young ones, I can see how this race and their silent speech with ancestral memories is very successful. I get the sense that novel situations are a little more difficult for them. By the way, have they said when the cycle might end?"

"It usually lasts for one full moon cycle, but here is the scary part, it's already been more than three months. They can't explain that, and the elders are very worried that the predation continues.

"I feel like we are living on the edge of disaster. One of these times a Great Raptor is going to catch us unprepared and that will be the end of us!" Amanda shuddered.

"I know, I've been having dreams every night about just that. I don't think we could ignore such a clear threat. I suppose all we can do is take extra care from here to Base Camp."

Amanda rolled over so that she was facing Jamie, "But what after that? Do you think they have fared better than us?"

"Tomorrow we will know more..."

Jamie might have continued but Amanda sat up, pulling her tunic over her head. In the fire light he stared at her naked torso, and all thoughts of Raptors faded.

---

Amanda shifted to a more comfortable position on the stone floor of the great cave. For most of the morning's exchange, Alheeza had been telling tales about how they had used their weapons to defend against both wilda-cats and mountain-wolves. The denzels marveled at these stories.

She listened intently as the elders summarized recent events in their culture. Apparently, their numbers had been shrinking due to violent attacks from the Great Raptors. This predation cycle had been far worse than any previous ones. The biggest problem the Denzels now faced was a dwindling population. Their very existence might be in danger. Jamie and Amanda's intervention the previous week was seen as hope for their future. This was a tangible bridge between their differing species.

It was the same group of elders that they had met the first day. What had changed was the way they sat, interspersed in a circle of inclusion.

Jamie addressed Alazar: *What news do you have of the others like us, the ones we refer to as Base Camp? Surely, some of your race have observed them before coming to the great denzel gathering.*

*You are correct, some denzels from the north have observed your Base Camp and have reported that, unlike you, they have not learned to live in harmony with our land. We hear they are like a blight, and I would not have welcomed any of them. You and Amanda have changed my view of your kind, but, as for Base Camp, I remain unsettled and reserve judgment.*

Taking a moment to digest all that was said, Jamie continued, *This is very bad news to us. We had hoped they survived without losing their thinking machines, but obviously they are suffering terribly. It is my intention of continuing our journey, with Base Camp as our destination. There are family members there whom we want to see very much. I understand your trepidation, and ask only that we pass through your lands to evaluate their current situation. At least you know that Amanda and I have the greatest respect for your race and its culture.*

Amanda had been listening to all and she added: *If they can learn what we have learned, maybe there is hope for our species to cohabitate.*

Alazar cast a stern look at her: *Amanda from the Stars, I understand your hope, but let me say this; I hold no hope unless you can bring back very real proof of a change of heart.*

*That's fair,* telepathed Jamie as he rose.

# In Search of Base Camp

A cool wind swirled their hair as Jamie and Amanda stood shoulder to shoulder, dressed in their handmade clothing. They stood on the last ridge of the mountain range that divided the land. Unlike the forest they saw on the other side, the hills that ranged away from them seemed rugged with twisted tree-like growth in the low and shaded areas. All else was relatively bare, and perhaps their traveling would become easier. In the four days since leaving the gathering, the five travelers had trekked over some very difficult terrain.

Anness, one of the two guide denzels that came from these hills, mind-spoke: *Your Base Camp is two more sun cycles from here. When my mate and I last observed them, one moon cycle ago, most had not ventured more than a half sun cycle from their strange contraptions. The few that ventured farther ran into wilda-cats, their deaths have kept the rest from ranging too far. If they had made it to the edge of the hilly plateau, things may have turned out differently. That is where it opens up to the coastal plains rich in food stuff. Most of our race come from there.*

Amanda telepathed: *It does not sound as if our people have fared very well at all. What about tonight's campsite?*

Anness responded: *There is such a place not much farther ahead.*

Jamie leaned on his spear, *Good, I don't want to take extra risks beforehand.*

Alheeza mind-spoke: *What do you expect when you meet with members of your kind?*

Jamie rubbed behind his ear as he mind-spoke: *That is hard to say. It seems a life time since I've been away, but I know it is not so long really. Nevertheless, so much has changed for us. I still miss Symone, my viss-comm implant, but life without the technology is getting easier and easier. From what Anness observed, I fear that my peers may not have made the transition as easily.*

Amanda absently rubbed her own node, staring off into the hills. She wondered what the people at Base Camp would think when they saw how she and Jamie were dressed. She smiled to herself, feeling more pride in what they had been able to achieve. The three of them had done well as a team. She knew the worst of their trials were behind them, or at least she hoped they were.

A flock of ground cover feeders took to the air as they descended the hill. Their ragged cries grated on Amanda's ears, in contrast to the beauty of their bright blue and white markings as they flapped away.

---

Following his guides, Jamie pushed himself to climb the steep slope, his pack and gear flopping as he wove his way past the twisted trunks of the purple-leafed trees. Going had been slower than he had hoped. Just as he started to doubt that the ridge was near, he broke over the top. The foliage gave way to a ground cover that came up to his waist. The denzels were standing precariously on their hind legs, looking ahead. From his vantage point Jamie could see there was something unusual in the valley ahead.

Amanda came puffing up beside him. "What do you see?" she asked.

*I can't tell; it looks different from what I remember. There was a wide valley, but I did not look too closely at the vegetation in those days. This could be it, but I don't remember that long trench and where are all the tulip shelters?* mind-spoke Jamie.

Unconsciously, Amanda clutched her amber stone: *And where are the skimmers?*

*We saw activity as little as a moon cycle ago,* added Anness.

Jamie squinted into the distance, trying to make out the details below. Where the neatly aligned white shelters should have been, there was only scattered debris along the scarred landscape.

*I see movement at the far end,* broke in Alheeza.

Sure enough, small figures were moving toward a large mound far off at the end of the trench. They moved like people but at more than a kilometer, it was hard to tell. As he studied the large area, the low sun caught something shiny on it.

"It has to be manmade," Jamie whispered to himself.

Amanda pressed against Jamie, and in a hushed tone added. "If you ignore the clutter around the perimeter, it looks a lot like the cargo shuttle, doesn't it?

As if a veil had been lifted, Jamie realized what he was looking at. Just as it had been with their damaged skimmer, a deep furrow scarred the landscape leading to the crash site. The big difference was this one dwarfed theirs. At the end of the ragged trench lay the crippled remains of the once proud cargo vessel. It was half disguised with debris piled up around it, but the shape was still unmistakable.

They stood there without speaking. Finally, Jamie mind-spoke: *This proves the worst of my fears, all of our neuro-electronics failed at once. We are well and truly marooned here.*

*Was that not your fear all along?* mind-spoke Amanda.

*Sure, I feared as much, but seeing is believing.*

*Shouldn't you seek out your kind before the sun sets, my friend?* Alheeza added.

*Yes, let's hurry,* telepathed Jamie.

Anness mind-spoke: *We are reluctant to come closer. My mate, Toobya and I, will watch from here.*

Jamie looked at Alheeza wondering if he would choose to stay back with the others, but he stepped forward mind-speaking: *We have come this far together, I will come with you.*

Amanda could have hugged him.

Jamie strode off down the slope, using the butt of his spear as a walking stick. He felt his pulse quicken at the thought of seeing other people after all this time.

Amanda and Alheeza followed close behind.

She was tired and had been hungry for so long that she paid no attention to the gnawing in her stomach. "Come; let us make ready for the darkness," she said in a rasping tone. The five ragged people around her started to shuffle towards their shelter.

She scanned the horizon for danger, her steps faltered as she detected movement at the edge of the trees. Three creatures, two tall and one shorter, were making their way down the ridge, and they seemed to be coming towards them. Fear rippled down her spine. There had been too many ugly surprises already on this desolate planet.

"Quickly people, danger approaches!" She pushed her body to move faster, but it was only a little faster than a shuffle. Starvation had taken a terrible toll on all of them. Even with their best effort she could see that the newcomers were going to intercept them before she could make for safety.

Within a few minutes a human voice called out to them, "We have come looking for survivors at Base Camp."

Jamie could see the lead figure halt, turning towards them. Almost running now, gear flapping, he called out again, "This is Base Camp, isn't it?"

At these last words the lead person seemed to stumble. Quickly, he closed the gap with the collapsed individual. He or she was in dirty tattered clothing, and as he squatted alongside, he could see the individual was very thin, worse than Amanda had been when he found her. A boney hand drew its brittle tangled hair away from the filthy face. Sunken but intelligent eyes looked up at him and a thin raspy voice said, "Who are you?"

Kneeling, Jamie continued, "I am Jamie Chambers and I have come looking for my mother."

Tears formed and her thin lip quivered as she said weakly, "You can't be, he and my husband were lost months ago. None of the surveyors have ever come back."

"Mom?" he said, as tears welled up.

"Jamie?" she said as tremors shook her body. She stared at him for some time before continuing, "You look so different with a beard, your strange clothing, and is that a spear? You look like some sort of caveman, reborn." She raised a hand to his face, adding, "And you look so healthy."

"That is a long story, I'll tell you later," said Jamie as he carefully lifted his mother, drawing her into a tender embrace. Their bodies heaved as they cried together. Neither heard the arrival of Amanda and Alheeza, who stood at a discreet distance opposite the other bedraggled people.

Margery pushed back far enough to see her son's face. "Where is your father?"

"Mom," Jamie's voice cracked, "He fell off a cliff into a river, where he died. I found his body later."

That started a fresh wave of crying. Finally, Margery whispered, "I loved him, you know!"

"So did I…."

They just rocked, holding each other for some time.

"What happened here, Mom?" Jamie asked in hushed tones.

She leaned back, looking up into his clear blue eyes. "Everything went wrong. All the systems failed, and then the cargo ship crashed right into the settlement killing almost eighty people. We thought that was the worst, but it has been a constant battle to stay alive. This seemingly innocuous planet, has been trying to kill us ever since. The big black flying things that come at night are the worst; we have lost dozens more to them." Her head sagged, and then with a wheezing breath she looked up into her son's eyes, "Then the supplies started to run out. That was nearly a month ago. We are almost dead for lack of food and clean drinking water."

Jamie reached around his pack pulling his drinking jug free.

As he passed her the jug she asked, "What's this?"

"It's just good clean drinking water Mom."

He helped hold it as she took a shaky sip. Pausing to take a breath, she gasped, "Oh, that is so good."

*The light is going my friend. Time to find shelter for the night,* mind-spoke Alheeza.

"Where do you stay at night, Mrs. Chambers?" asked Amanda gently.

Margery looked, seeing the young woman for the first time. As their eyes met, she asked, "Who are you?"

"I'm Amanda Martin."

"Amanda Martin?" Margery whispered. "You weren't with Fingland and Jamie."

"No, my mother took me surveying, like so many others. Jamie saved my life after my mother was killed by the Great Raptors."

"Oh, I am sorry to hear that. When we left Earth, your mother and I were friends."

"I remember you from the Mayflower; you were always very nice to me."

As Margery spoke, Amanda took out a sliver of copeander fruit. She passed it to Jamie's mother saying, "Here eat this, you will feel better."

Margery looked at the wrinkled wedge only for a moment before putting it in her mouth. After she chewed and swallowed, her eyes seemed to brighten. She remarked, "You look so different now. I would never have recognized you either." Margery looked her up and down. "Where did you get those outlandish clothes? And you look so healthy. How can that be?"

"I made them. The rest of the story that will have to wait."

Jamie's mother looked over her shoulder toward the derelict vessel. That is when her eyes met Alheeza's. She jerked with fright at the sight of him.

"It's OK Mom, this is Alheeza. He is a friend that I met on this planet. I would not have survived without him."

Margery turned to look back at her son, fear traced across her face.

Jamie continued, "Really it's all right; he very much looks like the dogs of Earth, just smarter."

*A dog? Are you still calling me a dog?*

*I am still making this up as we go along. Be patient, this should work out.*

"Mom, where do you take shelter at night?"

Margery turned and looked back to the crippled transport vessel where a number of slender figures could be seen lurking just beyond the debris. "We hold up in the ship every night, the tulip shelters that were not destroyed in the crash were smashed by what you call Raptors."

"Then we had best get under cover before full darkness," said Jamie.

# From the Darkness

—————◯—————

As they approached the vessel, it became clear why they didn't recognize it at first. The crash must have sent dirt and debris into the air, some of which still covered the once shiny craft. The survivors had dragged parts of their shattered settlement to pile against the hull for reasons Jamie could not understand. As he cast his eye along the fuselage he saw the distinct claw marks of the Great Raptors etched across the exposed surface. Death had visited this place on dark wings.

It appeared that the entrance had been crudely fortified by a crisscrossing of shelter segments intermingled with discarded storage containers and equipment. Despite Margery's weakness, she knew her way through the labyrinth by heart. She ducked and swung from segment to section as if in slow motion. Her group limped after her, followed by Jamie, Amanda and Alheeza.

*I can go no further. I will take up a vigilant station out here. I can hide within one of the containers,* Alheeza mind-spoke.

*That is probably for the best, we do not know what conditions are like inside*, telepathed Jamie.

*The light will be gone soon. I know that Anness and Toobya will make for the boulder field in the last valley. Let me know what your plan is. Until then, I will wait.*

*Sounds good, I will get back to you as soon as we have a plan. Thank you, my friend, we would not be here without you,* mind-spoke Jamie.

"Watch your step," croaked Margery. "You haven't had our practice getting in and out of here. Now, put out your hands and duck low here."

*What's that smell?* Amanda asked silently.

*I think it comes from the people inside,* Jamie mind-spoke.

Following Margery, they ducked through the portal where Amanda was hit by a wall of stench so strong she could hardly breathe.

What light was left in the evening was being swallowed by the depths of the transport vessel. Jamie blinked trying to make out something he remembered about the last time he was on this vessel. There was just enough light left to see a floor covered with suffering humanity, crowded on the slightly slanted floor. Amanda almost choked, not from the smell so much as from the sight of so much human suffering.

Despite all the time Jamie had spent in this cargo hold, nothing looked familiar. All of the interconnection storage containers had been stripped away, leaving a dirty metallic cavern. It was now the desolate refuge of the remnants of Base Camp. A wave of despair swept over the young man as he wondered how they would be able to help so many suffering people.

He broke the silence by asking, "How many are in here, Mom?"

"There are ninety-six of us still alive. One hundred six of us have perished, two since yesterday." Margery said.

"She-it!" muttered Jamie.

Slowly, he became aware of the low level sounds of coughing, and moaning mixed with the rustling of desperate people.

From the back, someone spoke up, "Who are these strange people?"

Margery turned in the dim light saying, "This is my son, Jamie, and Amanda Martin. They are the first of the lost ones to return. We should be thankful that two of ours have come back."

"Do they have any food?" someone else rasped.

"We have some food, but it must be shared with the weakest people first," said Amanda loudly, as she hoisted her bulging pack in the air.

At this the room was filled with many raised voices.

"Silence, all of you!" rasped Margery. Few seemed to listen.

Amanda passed her pack to Jamie, telepathing: *We need more light.*

Rummaging in her side bag, Amanda pulled the clear storage pouch free. Three shakes and the bio-luminescent creatures flew from their hiding place. A soft warm light pushed back some of the darkness.

The stark cargo bay fell silent in an instant. All eyes were turned upon Amanda as she held the glow globe aloft.

"How did you do that?" Margery asked in awe.

"It's something we learned on our way here. Aren't they beautiful!" replied Amanda.

"What she really means is that it's something she invented on the way here," Jamie said with a hint of a smile.

"It's like magic," said somebody close by.

"Yes, it is a bit like local magic," Amanda replied warmly.

Margery looked up into her son's face, now lit by this new wonder. "You look all grown up, so tall and look how you have filled out. I didn't know you."

"Mom, I have so many questions." He paused looking into the sunken eyes of his beloved mother. "When did you last have food?"

She looked down before answering, "Not since yesterday or maybe the day before that....." she trailed off.

*I gave her some copeander fruit. How about a few herman-nuts?* mind-spoke Amanda.

*Yes, why didn't I think of that? What about the others?* telepathed Jamie as he unslung his pack.

He passed his mother a couple of white nuts to chew while rummaging for more of the healing fruit. He found it in a side pouch of his pack. He unsheathed his glass blade slicing up a handful, before passing it to Amanda.

Looking down at Jamie, Margery asked, "Is that the wrinkled stuff you gave me out there?"

"We call it copeander; it is a fruit that grows in the higher forests. Its restorative powers are truly remarkable."

"How much of this do you have with you?"

"Not enough by the look of this group, but we can help the seriously ill," offered Jamie.

And so it was that the newcomers moved through the tightly-packed survivors, administering small doses of the restorative fruit along with small bit of nuts and roasted tubers.

As Amanda held the glow globe aloft, Jamie kneeled by a skeletal young man who was coughing uncontrollably. His tangled oily hair covered most of his thinly bearded face, but there was something in the grey eyes that struck a familiar note. "Robert!" whispered Jamie. Through the spasmodic bouts, the vacant eyes seemed to focus. He drew a ragged breath, "You're.....*cough*.....supposed to be...dead!"

"Yeah, well I'm not. Sorry to disappoint you, but here I am. Please chew on this bit of fruit."

It was hard for him to chew and swallow but Robert persevered, and his coughing seemed to ease and his eyes brightened. After a few steady breaths he said, "Why are you being kind to me, I never was to you?"

Amanda mind-spoke to Jamie: *This is the creep that used to make your life miserable?*

*Yes! Funny thing is I do not care about that anymore.* Shifting to common speech he said to Robert, "That's all in the past. Now it's about surviving here, don't you think?"

All Robert did was nod slightly as Jamie and Amanda moved on. It was hard to tell how much time had passed, night had fallen long before. When they had shared their meager supply of food, medicine and water around to most of the people, they retired near the entrance to talk quietly with Margery. Jamie gave a quick overview of the time with his father, the crash with its systems failure, and how they had initially survived. He did not give a full account of Alheeza's real involvement, just saying that the creature followed them. After the part about his father's accidental death, Margery began to cry again. With Jamie and Amanda on either side, they held her until the sobs passed.

He was well into the part of finding Amanda and their time at

Sanctuary when a large crash came from outside. Everyone within the derelict vessel jumped at once. Something big was trashing away near the debris piled at the entrance. Jamie grabbed his crystal, knowing before he touched it that he had missed the arrival of their worst nightmare. By the glow-globe he could see that the people were pressing back from the portal.

"Have they ever gotten inside before?" he asked his mother.

In a frightened voice, Margery said, "Yes, which is why we were piling up a barricade to stop them."

Jamie felt a wave of panic as he realized that there was no time to light a fire; furthermore, he had little fuel with him. What to do? He felt Amanda's hand on his arm. Looking over he could see the terror etched across her face.

*Jamie, what now?* she telepathed.

He could not find words of comfort. The light from the glow globe was dimming as the occupants returned to their tiny nest. The crashing sounds grew louder, and the cargo vessel shuddered as if hit by a large object. Razor talons scraped overhead along the bulkhead, sending a high-pitched screech through the vessel. As he clasped his amulet, it started to glow red. His crystal-enhanced night vision, once such a comfort, now gave him a view of something terrible tearing at the entrance.

"Mom, you and Amanda should get as far back as possible!" he hissed.

His hand groped for his weapons. Whether it was conscious or not, Jamie found his flinger in his hands. With shaking fingers he notched a glass tipped arrow. The hull of the transport ship shook as several heavy blows tore at the overlapping debris. Red eyes appeared through the last of the beams followed by a reverberating scream. The horrible stench of its breath flooded the hull.

Jamie stood with his back to the bulkhead. He sensed, as much as he saw, that the attack was from more than one Great Raptor. They were clawing away at the barrier with their teeth and talons. Suddenly, the overlapping beams shuddered allowing a giant black head to thrust forward. Its long neck thrashed from side to side, opening a space, to allow its bulky body to move closer. Its bellowing scream along with its horrid breath shook Jamie, making his eyes water. The attacker lunged forward, and Jamie raised his arm to meet it with his extended flinger, reflexively pulling the crude trigger! In that moment of compressed time, he was aware of the arrow blurring forward to embed itself deeply within the left eye of his assailant. The resulting bellow was unlike anything he had heard before. Its head smashed up into the ceiling breaking part of its cranial fin. With nowhere to retreat, Jamie pressed his back into the bulkhead as he watched in horror as the great beast thrashed its head about, narrowly missing him. The death throes grew weaker until the great beast's good eye suddenly went dim. Its head and neck slumped to the floor, where a large pool of viscous yellow blood began to form from its self-inflicted wounds. The massive night killer sprawled before him, blocking most of the exit. The sound of departing Raptors left a silence in the ship that was total.

Amanda shook the glow globe back to full light, bringing with it a group release of held breath. Before them, was the dead body of a Great Raptor. The huge head lay tipped on its side, gashes from its death throes had sliced through its tough scales. Dark yellow blood oozed from its wounds. Both swept back fins on its head and jaw had been broken. A tiny wooden fletched shaft stuck out of its bleeding left eye. The once horrible mouth lolled open allowing an orange tongue to spill out over broken yellow teeth. What had been a huge night flying killer was now just a horrible stinking corpse.

Jamie was shaking uncontrollably as Amanda put her arms around him.

"You did it, my love! You killed a Great Raptor," she whispered.

He dropped his flinger, embracing Amanda. While they stood there drawing comfort from each other, a murmur started to rise behind them. It grew into a unified outpouring of voice. Jamie turned to see arms raised with all eyes upon him. Tears welled up as he took in the cheering crowd of survivors.

# Unexpected Help

The near death experience of the Great Raptor attack left Jamie's adrenalin charged body shaking. Despite the waves of fatigue that threatened to overwhelm him, he needed to find Alheeza. Squeezing cautiously past the bulk of the stinking corpse, he emerged into dim moonlight. It felt better just being outside and away from the putrid confines of the wrecked transport ship.

Alheeza mind-spoke as he emerged from the battered cargo cube: *I heard and felt the battle within, it makes my heart soar to know that this one will not hunt again.* Squinting at Jamie, he continued: *I did not know they could be killed.*

Jamie's face twisted into his crooked smile: *I did not know that either. It was just a lucky shot, I think.* Looking more closely at his friend he continued: *Are you injured?*

*I am unhurt. Do you have a plan for what follows?*

*Not really.*

Jamie looked back at the damaged ship just as Amanda was squeezing out past the carcass and debris. He gripped his ruby crystal and closed his eyes. As he cast about there was no sign of a living raptor, near or far. It was as if the sky had suddenly emptied of all the hateful beasts. As he let out the breath he had been holding, the full fatigue of the evening hit him. Amanda was at his side just as he staggered.

Alheeza telepathed: *I will rejoin my kind to share what has happened here. I will be back soon.*

Amanda helped Jamie slide against the cube to the ground. Glancing over her shoulder she saw their four-legged friend trot out of sight. Looking around she realized that, in addition to the unused cargo containers, the Base Camp refugees had collected branches and limbs from the local trees to add to their barricade. It did not take long to gather enough kindling for a fire. Using Jamie's knife and their favourite fire making stone, she had a cheery campfire burning in no time. The dancing orange light, warmth, and popping noises soon drew others from the derelict transport.

Jamie awoke with his head in Amanda's warm lap. In the predawn, he could see dozens of people gathered around a generous blaze.

Amanda spoke softly, "It is the first time any of them have ever been warmed by a real fire. For some, this is the most comfort they have felt since the solar storm."

Next to them Margery spoke, "It is like a miracle having you back. Our lives were a waking nightmare, now there is hope."

Jamie smiled up at his mother.

The sky in the east was glowing pink, with a promise of a fresh day. No one seemed to notice the approach of another group. It was Jamie who sensed them coming. He rose to stand looking towards the horizon and the newcomers.

Amanda rose beside him, clutching her amber amulet. Immediately she recognized Alheeza approaching, but there were others that she did not recognize. *What is happening?*

*They are coming.*

*Who?*

*All of them.*

*All of them who?*

*All of the denzels of the area are coming to help.*

Turning towards the people, Jamie said in a firm voice. "People, there is something you should know." When all eyes were upon him he continued, "We have met one of the indigenous species and he is approaching with more of his kind. Do not be afraid, these beings are here to help us."

A low murmuring grew around the fire.

With the brightening sky, Amanda could see dozens of strange denzels, with Alheeza in the lead, making their way towards Base Camp.

*How are we going to explain this?*

*I do not think this needs much explanation, see!*

Each denzel was carrying something in its mouth. Amanda recognized the delicious tubers from the forest carried by some, while others carried juicy swamp melons by their vines.

With mouths agape, the survivors looked on while Jamie and Amanda greeted these strange quadrupeds and took the food from them. Quickly the food was cut into sections and distributed.

Juice dripped from Margery's chin as she bit into the soft melon. It had an odd taste at first, but as she chewed and swallowed, it became sweeter. She looked over at her son, who was moving among the survivors, making sure each one had a wedge of melon and a chuck of the purple tuber to munch on. Her weathered face broke into a crooked smile.

Catching Amanda's expression she said, "What are you smiling at my dear?"

"Jamie smiles like you! I kinda like that."

Jamie strode past them returning to where the denzels sat watching the people eating their gifts. He crouched next to Alheeza, who was seated on his haunches, along with the others of his kind.

Jamie mind-spoke first: *I do not know how to thank you for the gifts of food and drink. These people are in a terrible state and this might just be what they need to encourage them.*

*In my opinion, it was the most direct way to open up communication between our kind. All of the time I have spent with you, has helped me see what you are capable of. It is my belief that we need each other equally. After all, you have protected many of my kind from the Great Raptors, and this is our way of giving back.*

Looking back at the survivors, Jamie continued: *These people will need a good deal of care and healing before they give much back.*

*I remember what Amanda was like when you first found her, these people will recover just as quickly with the right food and shelter.*

*Are you saying that you can take us someplace where that can happen?*

*Yes.*

*What is it like?*

*The lower delta, not more than a day away, is rich in food stuff and there is a set of shallow caves that our kind have used for many lifetimes.*

*That close?* Jamie sat up with a new feeling of vigor at the news. His gaze rested upon the dead raptor protruding from the battered transport. His brow wrinkled as the stench from the carcass drifted on the morning breeze. *We cannot stay here, that is for sure.*

*That is the truth.*

A fresh thought brought Jamie to his feet. His father talked about something he called closure. Now it was time to make some closure and move on! He was talking before the thought was fully formed, "People, we have just been made an offer that I think we should take very seriously. And there is a bit of tidying up that needs to be done before we can move on."

---

Fat sizzled off the stinking carcass as the flames licked about the dead raptor. Like an omen of changing times, a pillar of black smoke rose high into the sky, where it could be seen from a great distance.

Standing at the edge of the valley, it was a sight they would never forget. Amanda and Jamie had stopped to gaze back upon the pyre, where the hungry flames turned the flesh of their most dreaded adversary into charred remains.

Looking at the faces around them, there was no sign of regret in leaving this forlorn site.

Speaking more to himself than the group around him, Jamie said, "We'll come back to strip some of the precious metal later, but for now let's follow Alheeza and his kind to a better place."

Hoisting their makeshift travois, with a weakened survivor, they turned with the others to follow the denzels to the promised delta.

### The End

# NIGHT OF THE RAPTORS

Book 2 of the Mind-Speaker Series

A Novel

by

W. James Dickinson

# Out of Darkness

———————◯———————

Τ he prime hunter drew himself up, unfolding his massive leathery wings. For such large creatures their departure from the darkened cliff was almost soundless. Their black shapes cut across the star field as they made their way towards a small opening in the forest.

Mandu staggered as the room around him dissolved into the dark landscape where four huge creatures took to the sky. As quickly as the apparition appeared, it was gone, leaving him shaking.

His uncle Almar, turned to him asking, "Mandu, you look like you have seen a ghost!"

Mandu looked into his uncle's concerned eyes. "It's nothing really, probably just exhaustion from my manhood ceremony today. I'm really tired, that's all."

"Are you sure?"

"Yah, I'm fine, really!" Mandu answered, with more confidence than he felt.

"If you say so, " Almar paused while studying his nephew, "Alright then, let's finish getting you dressed because there is a party outside and they all want to meet the young man of the day. After all you will be called Mandeler from now on, and counted among the men in our community."

Moments later they stepped out into the yard, illuminated by dozens of glow globes. Mandu stopped to look towards the south-eastern horizon. Could there be something terrible coming from that direction? A cold shiver ran down his spine before he turned to follow his uncle.